A Wyrms Tale

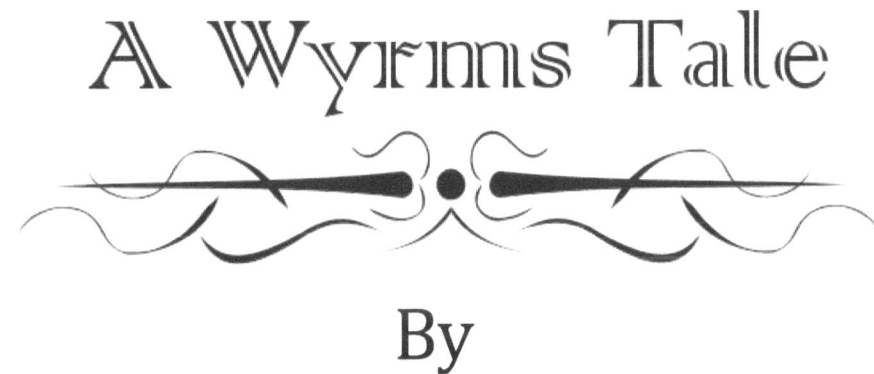

By

R Kane

Book one of The Paracletus Saga

A Wyrms Tale

By R Kane

Create Space Edition | Copyright 2016 R Kane

http://www.rkanepublications.com

This book is for my dear sister and brothers who were more important and inspiring than they ever knew...

THE LANDS

THE ENDLESS WASTE

the blood peaks

the forlorn mts

the argentum mts
(home of the fairrowers)

the cloudbreaks mts
(home of the urst)

THE VAST PLAINS
(home of the cairns)

hivego

gobara

thiathu swamp

thesedeu

Prologue

She rushed down the passage in a controlled panic with long strides of her short legs, which was not her normal demeanor at all, but for Hibbot the only choice left to her was to flee her home these last thirty years this very night. A large army of Anthros, all the Five Races of the Lands, from the Primates of the South to the Ursi of the high mountains, had gathered that midday out beyond the gates of Pallator and it was only the beginning to the nightmare unfortunately. It was not the thousands upon thousands of armed soldiers which had come to destroy the castle and deprive the ones who lived here of their lives which worried her, it was the soldiers inside warring against each other that did. All around, every corner and nook of the castle, the screams of the warriors who inhabited this once mighty fortress fought sword to sword, blows echoing with ear splitting clatters. The wails of death came from the darkened halls and passageways in shrieks, and all the noise of the battle thankfully deafened the sound of the crying young one packed safely in the sling around her shoulders. He had no name yet this little one being so new this world and here his only protector was old Hibbot, his human nurse maid. It was not the way one of his lineage should have been greeted upon birth, a grand celebration should be sweeping through the halls of the castle with cheers of jubilation...not the cries of agony from fighting. Smoke began to roll and swell along the smooth stones of the ceiling of the passageway thickening with each passing moment, the good air in the hall fading as the thick fog grew and overtook everything. She coughed low trying to keep quiet while forcing the bad air from her lungs as the babe in the sling strung across her abdomen cried even louder. Hibbot moved the cloth gently to the side to check on her charge, the small bundle squirming as she looked in on him. His eyes were closed in an intense effort at holding back the acrid sting of the air and he was breathing still, though with labor like she had too.

"We will be free of the castle walls soon little one, old Hibbot will see us out. You have no worries now, save for the large army gathered outside which has come to crush us." She whispered rubbing the boy's cheek.

He was not all human this child she was ordered to keep safe and neither was he a full member of any of the species of Anthros from this world. He was not a Simian from the great forest of the South Lands or an Equine from the wide plains of the West Lands. He was surely not an Ursi from the foothills of one of the tall mountain ranges to the north or one of the 'Burrowers', the Mustelidae who live high in those same mountains in their caves. He was neither feline nor canine which meant he was not one of the Daes of the East. And yet, when she stared at him in his swaddling old Hibbot could see all the species of the Magna Societate, the 'Great Society', staring back. He is an amalgamation of us all, Hibbot thought rubbing the pudgy cheek more savoring the soft skin and just the hint of the start of soft fur growing there. He was a piece of Simian and Equine, a small bit of Burrower and Dae, a touch of Ursi and yes, even a smidgen of human. He is all of us because he is meant to protect all of us. He is one of the unmatched warriors of this special race of men and women, born to the ones who protect this world we all call our home. He was one of the rare 'Paracletus' and all were supposed to look to him with awe, inspiration sweeping into everyone's hearts at a glance. Only now, his family was gone and his special kind, they were killing themselves all throughout the castle, brother killing brother and sister taking sister's life. The followers and workers here at the castle Pallator, the helpers in the kitchen and the smiths out by the stables, all were dead now as well.

The age of the Paracletus was closing and in a fiery end to it all.

"You will be just like your mother and father little one. Old

Hibbot can see you were meant to rule, yes she can. You have her wisdom and his strength and one day you will need the spirit of both to guide you. One day you may return to this old castle Pallator and may it be a better day than the end of this one."

Hibbot closed the sling and began once more to slip down the passage quiet and unseen as again all around her the world fought and came to a bloody end. Time passed without notice as she had just one task to which she focused all her attention, all her energy, and that was fleeing the blood stained walls of Pallator. There was secret entrance which led to the halls below and then the outside, only certain followers and the Paracletus themselves knew of this way in and out of the castle. It was meant to be an egress to allow access for the soldiers to take back the fortress if it fell into enemy hands, which was foolish if one considered the fact there was no army which could defeat the Paracletus. No, no human or Anthros force or army could breach these walls or dispatch these warriors, the indomitable Paracletus, and yet here were these unsurpassed soldiers falling to the one enemy no one could defeat. Finally, up ahead, as the din of the fighting in the castle began to reach a fever pitched crescendo Hibbot came to the last and the most dangerous part of her plan to escape. She silently came to a stop by the turn where this corridor she was in intersected with a small passage and looked down it. The small crossing led into an expansive chamber, the 'Great Hall of Pallator'.

On any day save this one the sight of the assembly room would bring a person to stop to take in its simple grandeur. The halls of the old kings, before the First Cataclysm, were said to be so grandiose it bordered on being obscene, rare gems and metals lining every surface one could touch was nothing but a sick covenant to greed. The old kings committed such acts to show their stature Hibbot thought as she began to slowly move down the connecting passage. They wanted all who entered their presence to be amazed, to be awe struck, and to be reminded of whom they were these old monarchs. Yet, where the old kings sought to strike one into submission with opulence, the Great Hall here at Pallator was meant to draw visitors in, to set them at ease. The Lord Supremes, the leaders of the Paracletus, knew their reputations would unnerve, even frighten, those who came seeking their aid so they made sure where they met the ones they protected was inviting and warm. These were humble soldiers the room said, extraordinary men and women who were just as normal as those they protected. There was no gaudy gold inlay or shiny silver, no rare gem to reflect one's image. Even though the ceiling of the Hall was high overhead one could still see the large wooden beams that crossed and supported it, long large tapestries hung down from those beams in warm vibrant colors drawing one's eye instantly. Along one wall art hung in simple frames depicting well known scenes from the long celebrated history of the Paracletus while along the other hung portraits of former Dominum Summum, the Lord Supremes, and their companions. It was all meant to show anyone coming to the Hall these warriors were one with all the Races of the Lands, from the noblest to the lowest.

"Not this night," Hibbot whispered as the sounds of fighting were now ear splitting and the closer she approached the Great Hall she could see the Paracletus fighting. They were so fast her eyes could barely keep up with their movements, but with the loud clangs of weapons crashing into one another and the battle cry's old Hibbot watched in despair as she came to a stop by the end of the passage.

It was not supposed to be like this, it was not supposed to end this way Hibbot knew. These men and women, they are our protectors, our heroes who would hold back the evil from the Endless waste of the North. They were supposed to be putting an end to the vengeful Odi and the vile Trolls and hateful Ogres, not each other. They were supposed to stand as one against the cruelty of the Giants and not facing each other at sword point, and yet she watched in horror as the ones she had come to serve and love died at their own hands. The only light in the Hall came from the fireplaces along the walls giving a low light exposing a number of men and women, all facing one another, circling in what was to be a final stand. They spoke not a word as eyes were locked on another while hands gripped and released the pommels of swords and hammers. Oh please no more, old Hibbot begged silently, please no more death. Can you not see what has been done this night? Her pleas though were never answered, there would be no mercy given. If not with from each other than certainly not from the army of Anthros on the fields outside the walls of Pallator.

"Gareth would lead us all to our deaths at the hands of the armies of the Societate! Hirall was right to confront him and take the Summum Dominum from him!" A man suddenly screamed at the others across the circle, who only howled back.

"Hirall lies! Gareth is our Summum and would never have lead us in open war against the Anthros! He was beguiled by an evil which Hirall has a hand in!" A woman Paracletus countered with unyielding loyalty while pointing with her short sword and as soon as she was done the man next to her added his own anger to the fire.

"Hirall is a traitor, just look at the Anthros and their army gathered at our gates and tell me it is not the doing of the Vicegerent?"

The words were barely done before one of those loyal to

Hirall countered. "It is not the crazed words or actions of the Vicegerent Hirall which brought the wrath of the Anthros to Pallator. It was Gareth, his accusations and threats to the Races, and the time for talking is done!"

The nursemaid's breath caught in her throat as the confrontation came to the only conclusion it could, a bloody charge. The man with woman from before gave a war cry and in a blink charged, his sword in one hand and small axe in the other moving so fast Hibbot could not follow. She only heard the loud clang of his weapons striking into the steel sword of the one he attacked, the counter stopping the attack for a mere moment. Then everyone was fighting, striking at each other, and Hibbot knew she had to go now, in the chaos of the battle she could make good her escape. With steady legs and a will as strong as steel the nursemaid stood and without looking back darted out of the passageway and into the Hall. She made the first few steps without incident, but then two of the Paracletus, occupied so deeply with trying to kill each other, crashed into the wooden pillar Hibbot stopped by. The child in the sling yelled loudly at the one who was carrying him, but his wail was lost in the screams of all the warriors as the nursemaid jumped away from the hall support and ran for the other side of the room. Another pair fell to the floor, the man on top driving his sword through the chest of the one he knelt over. A look of utter joy crossed his face as

Hibbot gasped in horror, not at the man's expression but the blow from behind which cleaved his head from his shoulders in a spurt of blood.

"FOR GARETH," The lady Paracletus yelled proudly a moment before a large black mace struck her side with enough force to lift her feet free from the floor.

Hibbot backed away and turned to run just as she heard the mace strike again, maybe it was the end of the lady warrior and maybe it was not. The nursemaid did not think on the sound anymore. She only ran for the end of the Hall, for the secret passage she knew would be there. It was the only safe way out now, the fighting in the castle was too dangerous to try and stay. Hibbot had a charge she had to keep safe, a pledge to the lady Bryndul, the mother of the little one in the sling. He was special, the only one with the blood line of the Summum Gareth and as such he-

She did not hear the release of the bow string, in the din of the battle Hibbot never would have. She was not a trained warrior, there was little care given to being a warrior for the nursemaid even though she took care of an army of them day and night. No, Hibbot only felt the great pain of the arrow as it struck her back just a finger's width from the shoulder blade. She screamed and fell forward barely in control of her body for the last few steps to her destination. The pain from the missile flooded her brain and for a brief moment she lost concentration leaning up against the wall to gather her wits. Behind her the lady warrior who had attacked her fell to the spear of another Paracletus and he to the hammer of another. Hibbot slowly, painfully, twisted and walked away from the last of the battle in the Hall slipping away from the fighters. She found the secret passage, the sight of the hidden door slightly ajar giving old Hibbot a sense of relief which made her smile.

"See little one...old Hibbot will see us out...you'll see...yes...you will." She whispered over and over, weaker with each round, to her charge as her form disappeared into the dark of the secret passage. None followed because, unknown to the nursemaid, there were none left to follow her. The Great Hall was now no more than a tomb holding the bodies of the Paracletus who had fought to the death, no mercy asked or given.

"We have to leave Bryst. There is nothing left for us here but embers and betrayal."

How could he say such a thing the Lady Paracletus thought turning to look her companion in his deep green eyes? How could he abandon our people like this, our home? The questions must have been easy to see on her beautiful yet pained face. The long blond hair which fell down her back was singed in places from the fire and her face, a mix of all the Races like all Paracletus, was smudged with soot and blood. Her anguish must have been so evident, even through the grime and dirt on her face, to her companion that Treabor finally spoke edging close to her and speaking low, calmly.

"Gareth and Bryndul...they are gone my love."

"And how are you so sure?" She asked quickly, demanding to know how he was so doubtless of the dreadful statement. The lady warrior gave her companion no chance to answer as she twisted quickly and looked back to the castle watching it intently.

He shook his head as the Lady Paracletus behind them, the only one who made it free of the castle with them, spoke. Tears slowly fell down her stained cheeks as she pleaded. "You do not feel their spirit Bryst. I do not feel them any longer...the same as my Lothor. They are all gone now my friend...taken from us this night."

"Aveis speaks the truth Bryst," Treabor added quickly with his sweet voice pulling her back from the edge of the dark, "come my love, we need to see to our friend and her unborn child now."

"And what of their son, Gareth and Bryndul, do we leave him to be butchered or worse?" Bryst snapped feeling her heart break at sight of what was once so beautiful fall into ruin.

"I do not know my love, but I do know if there was a way to get him to safety then Gareth and Bryndul both would have seen to it. And I know now we must see to ourselves and our friend lest we fall like the others this night."

Oh I know, she thought this one called Bryst, they are both right...and yet I cannot leave with our Order like this. I cannot leave knowing it ended like this, killing each other in a bloodlust brought on by a malicious accusation born of some evil magic. Gareth had spoken so hateful with the envoys of the Races, so utterly hateful that she was sure he was under the spell of some Mage. It was why the Anthros were here now, to defend themselves and their 'Great Society' from the very ones who were supposed to protect them, only it would have never come to war. Gareth was about to meet with the rulers of the Races and end the confrontation before it began, only Hirall had played one last lie to keep that from happening. It is done now she thought, an end no one could have envisioned in the darkest of nightmares. Bryst turned from the sight of a burning Pallator, the windows filled with smoke and flame now. She could no longer look to her home burning and instead took her love's hand and looked into his eyes again seeking at least a small sliver of solace. When he smiled, even sadly, Bryst smiled back feeling a warm peace begin to push against the pain in her heart before she spoke to the Lady Aveis. "Are you hurt my friend?"

"In the physical no, but in my soul...I am alone my friend. My companion will not be here to watch his son grow, to teach him to be honorable." Aveis answered with a voice strained with sadness, cracking with anguish.

"Then let us help Lady Aveis, let us teach your child the ways of the Paracletus...let us teach him the ways of honor. Let this night not be our end but our rebirth." Treabor stated with such steadfastness it made the Lady Paracletus only nod. Aveis reached up and wiped away a long strand of brown hair from her beautiful face, the species of the Societate easily showing through, as Bryst walked up taking her hand.

"Yes, come with us my dear friend and let us teach him of his father Lothor...of our beloved Summum Gareth and his loyal companion Bryndul. Come with us and let us three teach him of our Order so he will know the truth and not the lies of this night."

Her words were strong and the look from her dark blue eyes fierce. Bryst gave her friend's hand a squeeze letting Aveis know there was only one true choice here. With a simple nod Aveis agreed squeezing her friend's hand in return. There was only one true choice this night and even with the pain of loss the Lady Paracletus knew this. So with the end here the two walked away from the area disappearing into the dark leaving behind the life they had both devoted themselves too, leaving behind the ones who they had loved so much. Only Treabor took a last look back, a short one with a slight sigh. It was done he thought, the dream and purpose of this...way...it was done...for now.

One

80 years forward...

"Why do you keep looking back there, behind us?"

The question had been asked a moment before and not yet answered, which is why the Fox asked it again. The lithe frame of Rehema stood as still as the Cypress tree next to her and she remained just as quiet as her yellow eyes scanned the swamp around the group with long slow exacting sweeps. The heat of the day was diminishing as slow as the sun's descent but the sweltering humidity's refusal to lessen one bit was as annoying as the flies which circled her lean fur covered body. She looked over every tree and bush, exposed root, and pools of water searching for what her instincts told her was there but her eyes could not confirm. It was not the fact the Serval Cat refused to answer the question from her companion and fellow thief Lalya, a sly Fox with short red fur and matching short ears, but simply Rehema knew not how to put into words what she was sensing. She crossed her yellow-spotted fur covered, and slender, arms under her bosom sighing low as she did while her eyes kept scanning and her long ears, each adorned with several silver and gold rings through the skin, listened intently for any sound that was not part of the swamp. Her long wiry tail even ceased its motions, as if the small jerking movements it made were a possible distraction. The leather armor she wore, specially treated and cured so as to be supple and quiet for the duties a thief with the 'Unseen Hand' were to perform, gave no sound or creak at her touch which aided in her listening for a sound at the moment.

"I think our friend has sensed someone...or something following us." A gruff voice answered low from behind. The Fox turned slightly to give her attention to the one who spoke and his dark brown eyes, a canine from the Daes of the East. Elas was just like other canine's, his maw prominent with large pointed ears, one pierced with rings of gold and silver. His fur was a dark brown with oblong black spots, which covered a well-muscled body or one could assume if his thick coat was not present. The only visible body parts the thief allowed into view were his arms from mid-bicep down to a pair of large four fingered humanoid hands covered in fingerless gloves and his long tail. Everything else was hidden in dark leather, the same as Rehema's, and a pair a light weight boots with no visible soles.

"Reh would have told us if someone was following," Lalya

answered before turning back to her friend the Cat, "you would have told us right?"

The Serval only nodded and sighed again frustrated in both having to cease her detection of the elusive feeling of being watched and for not being able to determine who or what was causing the unease she felt. Rehema turned just enough to look the Fox in the eyes as she spoke. "Of course I would have told you Lalya...and Elas as well even though I would have had to wake him to do so."

The remark, the end of it especially, was enough to break the tension for at least the foreseeable future. Lalya the Red Fox was the tough one among them, the protector of this little band of larcenous Anthros, from the day all three had met in the bazaars of Thesedell, the great Eastern city of the Daes. The Fox smiled and looked over to the Canine who shook his head and gave a small 'Huh' as he did. "Are you saying I am a lazy Dae?"

"Not at all my brother in the dark," Rehema smiled halfheartedly to Elas, "I just wish we could all sleep the day away dreaming of our loved ones back home, free of distractions."

It was hard not to sense the worry or see the concern on the Serval's face, her feline features prominent with the accent of spots from her fur. Lalya reached over and put her hand on her friend's shoulder and whispered with reassurance. "We will return with the gem Reh. We will give it to Scars as Kazmir ordered, and in doing so free Sefu your brother my friend."

"I know we will...it is just...have you not felt the presence of someone watching, someone out there in the swamp?"

Lalya stared at the Serval for a moment then looked over to the Canine who sighed then nodded before answering gruffly. "Yes, but just enough to make the fur on the back of my neck stand at end."

"Then there is something there, you both sense it?" Rehema asked quickly.

"Truth, yes, but we have not been able to discover what it is. We, Elas and I, we were hoping you would have found the mystery out by this hour." Lalya said shaking her head, the rings in her ears gleaming from what sunlight broke through the swamp's canopy of trees and vegetation. Her thick tail swishing from left to right disturbing nothing but the air.

"I have nothing to tell me what it is which is following or why." Rehema answered with a whisper still watching the swamp, still waiting for something to show. She was the one all four, when her brother was with them, looked to for counsel. 'You are the smart one sister, the one who we all follow without question' Sefu her brother had said once.

Please Mother, she prayed silently, let me be smart enough this time.

He lay perfectly still on the large tree branch staring back through the mass of leaves and moss at the Serval Cat with the same intensity in which she looked for him. Oh he knew she was looking for him, could 'feel' him just at the edge of her strained senses. There was no chance the cat would derive his spot among the trees though, he knew this as well. Her nose and ears were exceptional he could tell but no Anthro had ever or could ever detect his approach. So he sat there without worry examining the three as closely as he could, insatiable curiosity making it impossible to look away. The three all looked different obviously being different races and he took a mental note of each, of their varying and contrasting appearance. He watched every little movement of the trio feeling a strange kinship with them, all three.

He looked down at his own body, past the ramshackle jumble of leather's he wore to his body beneath, and knew those three down there and he were as close as blood would allow. He was all of them, part cat and canine and fox, the only question was how, why? He had fur covering his body, only not as much or as thick as the Anthros, any race of the five. He was tall, just at seven foot, like the Equines of the plains and well-muscled from his wide shoulders to his feet like the Ursi of the mountains. His face was shaped slightly like the Simians of the forest just northwest of here with a nose and mouth that protruded just a little and ears like a Canine's. His eyes, from what his sister and mother had told him, were always like the secretive cats and foxes of the east while his hands and feet were most certainly human with five fingers and five toes on each. Truth be told Jared knew little of the other Races with the exception of the generalities. When any would stop by the farm to do business or visit he would go and hide in the lofts over the stables as he was ordered. His mother would tell him it was necessary, a part of his life he would have to accept. 'No one must know you live here Jared, no one...ever' she had told him sealing it with a promise. It was probably why he was so curious when he came across any of the five Races wanting to learn as much as he could.

The thought of his family, not his true family but the one who raised him, brought an end to the studious studying he did of the trio of Anthros. Memories seemed to be the only thing that could stop the need to know who he really was, what he was. His name is Jared Sinn, the name given to him by the human woman he called mother, though she was not his true birth mother. The human woman's name was Poll and he was told later what he had already come to realize before that day, the truth that he was not her son and his sister Mallot was not his true sister. Poll's mother had found a babe while hunting for mushrooms in the forests one morning, a small wee babe in need of food and warmth. So Poll's mother took the babe in and raised it as her own at the little farm they lived on till she passed and then the duty of keeping the child, who was still too young to be left alone, fell to Poll herself who had married. She raised him alongside her own child watching with a smile as he grew into a young man. Jared had realized early on age that he aged slower, much, much slower than his mother and sister. When Poll passed Mallot asked him to stay on at the farm and he did so and before he knew it the roles of his life had changed, turned like the seasons. No longer did Jared need looking after but now he was the one looking after his sister who had never married.

Mallot left this world six year's past and before she crossed to the next realm she gave him one last gift, from his mother Poll. Jared reached into a small roughly hand sewn pocket on his tunic and produced a medallion, a coin almost in his hand. It was flat and smooth on one side while on the other a strange set of markings and an emblem were carved in the face. Mallot said it was on him, tucked in the swaddling, when their grandmother had found him so long ago, the only artifact that linked his unknown past to this known present. No one they had dared show the medallion to knew what the meaning of the markings was she told him with a wistful smile and none knew who the emblem represented, it was a crest for a family but what family his mother and sister knew not. He had no clue as to what the medallion meant, but Jared had curiosity and that was more than enough three weeks prior to send him in search of a special one to examine the disc, an apothecary and a weasel and an astute historian. She is a wise one this 'Burrower' a shopkeeper had told him in the wondrous Simian city of Gobara. She would most certainly know the writing on the medallion the human hissed low, so who better to ask he thought, who better to answer the burning questions in his mind.

And that, as the saying goes, was all he needed to hear. A simple conversation which set him on this fateful journey to the expansive Thathu swamp. One night, after travelling to a remote and small village further to the South of Gobara to meet with the apothecary and learn what the markings and the crest on the medallion meant, to learn who and what he was, yet Jared was not ready for what the Weasel told him, her sable fur shining from the light of the hearth. The words of the apothecary, a lone and mysterious figure who shunned the tunnels of the high mountains where other burrowers and the Ursi dwelled, bludgeoned him almost. This belongs to one of the fabled Paracletus she had told him with a smile, a sect of warriors with a...colorful past.

The Paracletus, he exhaled softly before leaning in, you think I am one of them. Oh Jared had heard of the master soldiers, warriors with unmatched skills in any number of weapons. His father, or the man he called 'Father', would regale him with tales of the exalted Paracletus, the protectors of the Races Jared whispered. He would tell a young wide-eyed boy how the soldiers had crushed the monsters of the Endless Waste, how when led by the Dominum Summum no army could withstand their assault. Oh he would, would he the weasel asked with a slight smile? Yes, he would tell stories and fill my head with images of these great warriors and he even told me once I could be as special as one of the noble warriors and now you say I am one of them Jared grinned. Is this what is carved into the medallion, the strange words, is that what this means? He asked and pushed the round disc toward her eagerly, almost too eagerly.

No, she quipped with a wave of her hand as he pressed her once more about the medallion, she did not know the markings or what those etchings meant but the emblem was part of the ensign of the fabled protectors. Jared sighed frustrated, his youth showing, and then she whispered low and mysteriously. There is one who could read the words on that medallion she had chuckled while smiling, one she knew of who could shed light on the mystery of those words, though the journey would be dangerous. Truly he had asked quickly and still with an eagerness which bordered on uncontrolled, is there someone who can tell me what this means? Jared my young lad, she grinned wider with mischief as the fire they sat by cast her sable face a fiery red, you just have to show the courage needed to enter a certain cave and ask old Thaxmosis himself what those markings mean. What is a 'Thaxmosis' Jared had asked back with a whisper and the weasel's answer shocked him to his very-

A sudden noise brought his attention back to the trio of Anthros he had been diligently watching just a moment before. Now the three were joined by another trio, and Jared gave a small snort voicing his displeasure with these new people.

"Why does she keep looking behind us like that?"

The question by the human thief Baldric was more sneer than inquiry and it drew no answer from the Anthros, who were coming close to having their fill of the three humans who had come along on this journey. Kazmir, through his emissary named Scars, had forced the addition of Baldric and his ilk. It seemed having Rehema's brother as a captive was not enough insurance for the master of the thieves' guild of Thesedell so Kazmir sent along Baldric and the brothers Rolft and Fendrel as his eyes while the Anthros retrieved the gem. The group was barely out past the gates of the Dae city before they were threatening each other, and there was more to the dislike and harsh words than just the obvious disdain for each other. Lalya had told Rehema of rumors and shadowy chatter among the other thieves that Baldric was secretly in communication with one of the 'Red Remnant', the ones who were left of the infamous Assassins Guild called 'The Red Blade'. Dark and sinister were the humans and Anthros which filled the ranks of that brotherhood Rehema knew, an evil without any kind of leadership or guidance which meant it was just waiting to unleash itself on the city of Thesedell and its unsuspecting citizens. Years ago people began to disappear, no one of worth at first which kept the search for the missing terse, but then more and more prominent men, women, and Anthros began to go missing in the wealthier parts of the city. Well, when the rich began to go missing it was not long before the vile reputation of The Red Blade started to spread like pooling blood around the Dae city of Thesedell. The peril from the Assassins Guild was so clear and bright it caught the attention of the Leo and Mastiffs themselves, the dual rulers of the Daes. The Pride and the Pack moved swiftly and crushed the Blade with an iron clawed fist killing or imprisoning any guild members it found, yet as always some escaped into the night. Those who did now laid low in the lower parts of the city hiding among the shadows with the outcast and castoff. The Red Remnant was just as dangerous as its father the Red Blade because, as everyone knows, when you corner an animal that is when it becomes its most dangerous.

"Why not ask her yourself Baldric? Being in the middle of your discord gives me a head that aches uncontrollably." Elas hissed while pulling out a dagger to polish and sharpen.

The remark drew a scornful look from the brothers but Elas just ignored them, truth be told there were few humans that scared him. Baldric eyed the Canine hard before turning back to Serval sneering again. "Do you sense someone following us?"

Rehema refused to answer the human leaving the question hanging in the air between them all. The withholding of a response was just another slight in a growing number for Baldric and soon, very soon, he would set those scales to his favor. For now, though, he kept his dark desire for satisfaction to only himself as he growled. "Is there some-"

"Nothing behind us concerns me Baldric," Lalya suddenly spoke up trying to take the hateful eyes of the human off her friend and placing them squarely on her, "not as much as that which lies ahead of us, between us and the gem."

Baldric refused to take his eyes off the back of Rehema's

head even as the Fox confronted him, staring at the Serval maliciously for a moment longer before turning to look at Lalya. He wanted the red furred fool to know he followed no one's orders but Kazmir's, and that was only when it did not interfere with his needs. "Are you afraid of what the legend says lives in the cave Anthro? Are you scared of the tales of an ancient dragon guarding the gem?"

"I am concerned as to what we face to retrieve the gem, be it dragon or some fool human who likes to talk too much. I do not like entering a place I have not studied Baldric, and with you following from behind as I hear you always do...that ominous feeling only grows more." Lalya hissed back letting her words cut the thief deeply.

And her words did as Baldric hissed like a snake from the rebuke, the sneer turning to a snarl with a flash, yet he was not the one to attack. No, he left that to his henchmen Rolft, a vile looking human who bathed with rarity it seemed, or so the nose of the Canine Elas told him. "You callin' us cowards' lady?"

"The lady only states that which the man's reputation has already whispered," the Canine suddenly growled displaying his sharp teeth while standing up to his full six-foot height, "but if you would like to discuss your exception...I am quite free at the moment."

A fight was just a blink away from breaking out for the party, the humans' hands slowly inched toward the pommels and handles of swords and daggers. Elas held the dagger from before loosely but with the point forward, the tip ready to plunge into flesh, while Lalya slowly drew one of the two hand crossbows she carried at her back. Oh yes, blood was just a heartbeat away from being spilt, but then Rehema's voice broke through the tension bringing a quick cessation of hostilities for the moment. "Am I going to have to save my brother by myself? Truly, am I the only one here who understands where we, all of us, stand?"

Lalya and Elas both froze as their minds took the questions in and tried to access what their friend was asking. Baldric and the brothers, well the three just stood looking lost, just like they had been these last days of travelling. Rehema sighed heavily and strode between the feuding groups pushing past both her friends and stopping short of Baldric and the brothers by an arm's length.

"What good will we do killing each other out here in this swamp? Nothing that is what and my brother will be the one who dies for our idiocy." The Serval spat with disdain. Her words had barely ended though when the other brother Fendrel spoke finally.

"Your brother is a fool who deserves his fate for being caught 'working' in a city Kazmir the Rat runs."

Rehema sighed heavily again as the one idiot human clapped the other idiot human on the shoulder. Really, she thought, did these two sleep through the morning's events when Kazmirs' man gave them the order which sent them headlong into this swamp? "Do you two really see Scars or the Rat taking you back with any other feeling but anger if you return empty handed? Do you think Scars will just smile and let you live when you return without the gem?"

Oh, she had a point the worried looks on the brothers' faces stated as both suddenly grew quiet and with the momentum in hand Rehema only pushed more. "What were Kazmir's orders given to us by Scars Baldric, what were his words exactly? What order did he give you as Kazmir's Hand before we left?"

"Come back with the gem," Baldric whispered low chewing on his bottom lip after taking a moment to answer, "or do not come back at all."

And with that, with the realization the words brought, the Serval only shook her head as the brothers behind Baldric swallowed hard. Their faces no longer expressed a victorious visage but the worried one from before, just deeper. Rehema could imagine the look on her companions faces not needing to see either Lalya or Elas to know both were contemplating what was about to come. Still, with all their attentions now firmly secured in her grasp, the Serval only pressed her control, "now that we all have a better grasp on what we must do let us speak of how we will secure the gem."

"Come Elas, help me bind my tail while Reh talks," the Fox stated handing the Canine several long leather straps to tie off her long prehensile appendage.

So with a begrudging grumble Baldric let the Serval take over lead of the group. He did not worry though, oh no. He still had time to complete the true and secret order his soon-to-be Remnant brothers had given him back in Thesedell. 'Be the only one to return Baldric, with the gem in hand' the Second of the Red Remnant had whispered evilly as he smiled at him across the table at The Black Flower Inn. 'Do this and you will be one of us, the Master has graciously offered, but anything else will be considered a failure and you do not want that, I assure you' he had hissed. It was just a brief talk between the two, but it was enough for the man to make his intentions known, chiseled in stone you might say. So the animosity between the groups had almost come to a head and thus almost brought about a premature and unwanted end to his plan. It was not all bad though, this eagerness to kill each other he had just witnessed...it would come in handy later when the gem was in sight. For now, he just grinned and listened as the Serval talked, six were better than one and when the time came he would cut the cat's beating heart right out of her chest.

Whatever chances the six had of fighting disappeared quickly due the words of the Serval Cat Jared saw. The humans backed down quickly, with the exception of the middle one. He quit, but not because of what the Serval had said. No, Jared thought cocking his head to the right just a little while thinking on what he had just witnessed, this one has other business he is looking to finish. He has another set of secret plans all his own he thought. Jared felt a sudden need to try and warn the Anthros, to let them know this human was dangerous and one not to let wander without a close eye.

Yet he could not warn them. He was here on an undertaking of his own and that took precedence over anything else. They were all heading to the same place, to a cave rumored to be the lair of an old malevolent dragon. Why else would six thieves be in the middle of a swamp? So, if they were all headed in the same direction, why not use these six as a distraction to gain entrance into the home of this 'Thaxmosis'? The only problem Jared could see to his plan he told himself silently as he slid down from the tree limb just as quiet was what a dragon looks like these days. No one had seen one in so long, do the 'Immortalis Lacerta' still look like flying lizards? Jared readied what little gear he had brought, all that he owned really was put in place as he readied himself to enter the lair of the Ancient Dragon Thaxmosis.

Two

They were both old...so very, very old.

She could easily feel their age, the deific power and omnipotent essence manifesting off both as crazed as the idea sounded to normal ears. She could truly feel the limitlessness of the two Dragons who stood just feet from her and she shook just slightly from the awareness of it all. One stood tall on the grass of the glen, the small dark grey scales visible on the back of his neck and bald head, which throbbed with each breath as did the ashen skin that was not covered by long robes. The other, down on the grass in a half-sitting position leaning against the exposed face of a large boulder set half into the ground in the center of the clearing they stood, shuddered in forced breaths as he fought the poison which coursed through his body. His hair was gold, not yellow or sunlit, just flowing gold and his skin and scale tint was a bronze that came not from being in the sun but as almost part of the fiery orb itself which crossed the sky. She knew he was a protector, a true Gold Dragon. He was once a deep bright, stalwart color which stood strong for all those with good in their hearts to see, to be drawn too, but now...

"What are you doing Jura?"

The words were cold, so devoid of any emotion except evil that Jura knew instantly who spoke them, Thaxmosis. As she looked up from the Gold Dragon into those black eyes Jura shuddered uncontrollably. She hated being in presence of this old one, the hate and misery from his existence filled the very air around him threatening to choke her, leaving her unable to speak. Thaxmosis was just a hundred years short of being Ancient, so old he could remember when Dragons ruled the skies above these vast lands, from the North to the South. Old enough to remember none, not a living being, could challenge the might or the terror of the Immortal Wyrms.

"I was...watching you my lord." Jura whispered finally finding the strength to speak while lowering her gaze to her hands noting the tinted green skin and scales on the back of the appendages looked dull even in the light of the glen.

All Dragons, from wyrmlings to the oldest among the legendary beasts, now took the form and shape of the humans, or more like the Anthros. No Dragon could completely hide its real presence just as no longer were the skies filled with flying drakes terrorizing those below on the ground who were unfortunate to witness their flight, not anymore. The near demise of the

Immortal Wyrms came about due the Dragons and the race's own inherent weakness of hubris. Hundreds of years before the devastation of the First Cataclysm, the first great war between the Anthros and the Humans for the rule of the Lands, the Dragons fought their own internal struggle among themselves for the one who was supreme. Hundreds of years before the Paracletus destroyed themselves in a single battle of their own disastrous making the 'Immortalis Lacerta', the Dragons, tore their own world asunder. There were no sides Jura had been told by Thaxmosis one night not so long ago, there was no right or wrong in this war. There was just strength, the ones who lived were the ones who could not be taken or killed because those Dragons were too strong. The ones who lived on deserved to live Thaxmosis had grinned maliciously, as if a painful memory brought back some dark glee. Only, this civil war between the drakes had an unforeseen consequence he would hiss as he spoke. The Humans and the Anthros and even the Mythical Ones, all had grown in strength and in number while the Dragons had almost destroyed themselves. What few Wyrms remained could never fight them, all these new enemies to our kind, not even if we could band and become one Thaxmosis sneered while telling her. The Immortalis Lacerta were almost extinct, so few that the loss of any old one or young one would be devastating. So the Dragons hid, used their own magic to alter their bodies to what they were these days, a human-like being with scales, faces that were a mix of Wyrm with slightly protruding maws and chins, and a small tail sweeping from their backs. There were no wings, no fearsome bodies or claws, just these new bodies which could never be looked on as majestic.

Those days are gone Jura he had sighed sadly when he spoke of the past, the only moment the young Green Dragon had ever witnessed where Thaxmosis expressed even the slightest emotional vulnerability. He was black, in soul and heart and scale, so she had to wonder what it was that the old one missed so much.

"Are you certain Jura? Were you just watching or was there more? Maybe you were being drawn in by Palaxnym and his golden scales without realizing so?" Thaxmosis asked with a cold tone, the twin lengths of bone descending down from his chin like a human's hair.

She shook her head slowly looking up from her hands, "No my lord. I have been careful not to be deceived by Palaxnym as you warned me."

"We did not...we came...,"

Jura looked down to the one who tried to speak, the words addled and confused by the same poison that was quickly sending Palaxnym to a never-ending sleep. It was the Gold Dragon's companion, a slender blue version of herself. Only this Dragon was older by far, not as old as Palaxnym and Thaxmosis, but older then her and the other wyrmling in the glen.

"Oh yes Ith, this book, you came looking for one of my precious tomes?" Thaxmosis spat as he sneered at the Dragon laying on Palaxnym. "Do you expect me to believe you would risk a confrontation in my lair, with me, over a book?"

She was beautiful this blue drake, Jura thought as she stood quietly motionless. The grey robes she wore seemed to heighten the color of her skin and the black hair which ran down her back to almost her legs. Jura wondered how she had come to be in the company of the Gold, was she drawn to him like the stories of the days passed.

"Yes, for it is the truth. Palaxnym came looking for a tome he said you possess." A young but strong voice replied calmly.

Thaxmosis looked over finally to the last Dragon in the glen. He was young with dusky red scales, not quite Jura's age but close enough to pique his interest. He had been patiently waiting for another young one to cross his path; another Wyrm to take hold of and bring to his 'fold' you might say...and to his good fortune here was one. The fact he garnered this new young Wyrm while putting his enemy into a sleep so deep it would bring about his death, well that was just another reward for being so patient.

"What tome was he searching for?" Jura suddenly asked drawing a quick and contemptuous glare from her master.

Voarothim, the name of this new young one, smiled as his dark orange eyes locked onto Jura's yellow ones and he spoke kindly. "He said he needed to see a tome written by Cenloth the Mad."

"Cenloth," Thaxmosis abruptly laughed, the sound causing Jura to cringe involuntarily with the grating of it, "what would Palaxnym want with anything that crazed weasel of a historian might have written down?"

This is all over a book, both Palaxnym and Ith's suffering, it is all for a single tome Jura thought in horror. Dragons were hoarders of treasure, all Wyrms ancient to young and large to small felt the inexhaustible desire to attain precious metals and perfect gems, the boundless need to obtain rare magical items and then to keep it all hidden away from prying eyes and pilfering hands. Even Jura was allowed a small trove below, deeper in the caves. It was her own little pile that she would go and stare at, sometimes going without realizing how she arrived there, her body drawn involuntarily to the hoard. Yet centuries ago this desire, this need to have and possess treasure spread to knowledge, books and scrolls to be more precise. Dragons, old ones, began to accumulate aged and archaic tomes and scrolls and on rare occasion stone tablets. The Wyrms began to hoard the written words of Mages and other historians in vast libraries in their lairs. Dragons were forced from the land to survive and as an aftereffect the Wyrms became historians and observers of the events of the world. It was sad really Jura thought, what the Dragons had collected and now knew could help the Great Society only what would the Humans and Anthros do if the Wyrms were to reappear?

"I do not know old one," Voarothim answered never once stepping back from the obvious distaste of the old one. "We were in the mountains of the North observing the Odi during one of their rituals, a particular secretive clan, when Palaxnym overheard a conversation and he had to come here as quick as we could."

"Well, it does not matter really." Thaxmosis hissed taking one last look at the Gold and Blue Dragons before turning to leave the glen. He did not look to Jura knowing she would follow him dutifully but he stopped by the other Dragon. His dark eyes bore into the orange ones of this young one as he spoke. "By the time the sun outside rises tomorrow morning both Palaxnym and Ith will be beyond any revival."

"Why old one?" Voarothim asked with a questioning look.

The expression struck Jura as strange for the the moment she thought, so strange and out of place. Was he truly not concerned for Palaxnym and Ith?

"Why am I doing this you ask?" Thaxmosis grinned evilly exposing the rows of sharp teeth, ignoring the look from the young Dragon. "I am old young one and I achieved my age by being no fool. Palaxnym and Ith should have stayed away from my lair, stayed away from me and my books. Now they will sleep forever, poison I brewed just for any fool Wyrm coming into my domain being their demise."

Then the dark form of Thaxmosis was moving, heading for the edge of the glen in swift and uninterruptable steps. Jura looked Voarothim for a moment, just a glance, noting the questioning look was gone before both were turning and trotting after Thaxmosis. They never slowed as well as the old one walked straight into and through the trees. There was a moment when the image rippled and swam, just a billow as if a breeze had caught and twisted a tapestry. Jura went after her master stepping through the trees followed by the young Red Dragon who slowed a step, enough of a hesitation to steal the smallest of glimpses of the pair in the glen sleeping peacefully against the upturned stone. If Jura had seen this look she would have easily seen the concern in his eyes...but she was not here and thus missed it all.

The bright warm sunlight of the glen disappeared. It was replaced by the dark and the dank of a cave and when Jura stepped through the portal she wanted nothing more than to be back in the glen. She was a Green Dragon, born of the forest and nature. Even as fictitious and mocking as the scene in the magical space was, and Jura knew this to the deepest parts of her mind, she longed to be in that glen forever. Her soul yearned to fly among the trees and to lie in the grass and never leave. Yet, she was not allowed to stay. She was not allowed even a visit unless the old one was by her side, pulling the imaginary chain she wore round her neck, keeping her soul locked to his side, buried in this cave. Jura sighed heavily as young Voarothim stepped through the shimmering circle on the wall cast by the arcane device sitting on a shelf, the door to the magical space wavering like water on a pond. The young Dragon stopped and looked around lost for a moment then he saw Jura's beautiful face and just to her right was the gruesome visage of Thaxmosis. The old one was still grinning maliciously as his fingers reached down and closed the lid on what looked like a lantern sitting on the flat surface of a rock formation. As he did the doorway to the glen and to Palaxnym and Ith closed as well.

"Why am I here old one, that was the question I wished to

have answered." The young one asked abruptly. The tone of his voice was confrontation Jura thought with a twinge of fear, open and swift.

"Why are you here, Voarothim? Indeed, should not the question be more to the point of why have I spared you from the fate of the ones who were caring for you?" Thaxmosis asked back just as quickly. His eight-foot-tall form expanding just slightly in the chest, the sign he was accepting the challenge of the younger one.

Voarothim cocked his head to the right and opened his eyes just a bit. The question must have startled him Jura thought as the old one stepped up close enough to stare down on the young Dragon glaring with evil. "Yes, why am I not sleeping in that glen old one?" Voarothim whispered low conceding just as sudden as he had defied, to Jura's relief.

"There young one, knowing one's place is critical of survival." Thaxmosis whispered low like a hissing serpent. "I spared you the fate of Palaxnym because you my young friend are a dreaded Red Dragon and as one you are invaluable to me."

"What if I wish to leave?" Voarothim inquired slowly, carefully.

"I do not remember letting you have the choice of leaving

young one." Thaxmosis growled, his words coming from deep down in the center of his chest. When Voarothim gave no response the old one spoke on. "Here you will stay Voarothim, here you will stay and under my guidance and instruction you will achieve the impressiveness that is your lineage. Do you understand young one?"

There was a long moment of silence as Voarothim stared back expressionless to the last of Thaxmosis. Jura felt her heart lurch in her chest, the beat skipping and speeding out of her control. Please she wanted to say to Voarothim, do not fight the Terrible One. Yes, you will be a prisoner of the Great Black Dragon but is that not better than being dead? Then, as if the young Dragon had heard the silent plea, he nodded to Thaxmosis once again conceding, "Yes, I understand...my lord."

"Good, remember your place young one and grow." Thaxmosis said one last time before slipping away to leave the small cavern...or trying too. The tension was thick and it made Jura sick just a little, but then Voarothim spoke again.

"What is a 'Paracletus' my lord?"

That tension, which had flowed off Thaxmosis like foul air pervading the small cavern, swirled once more pushing on Jura's chest like a cold hand squeezing her heart causing her breathing to labor. She watched as the Black Dragon slowly turned back to the young Red Dragon snarling dangerously. "What did you say?"

"It is the word Palaxnym heard...my lord. He said the Odi were asking their old Gods in the ritual to keep their honored holy ones safe, the holy ones the humans referred to were 'Paracletus' Palaxnym said." Voarothim replied calmly, almost too calm Jura thought. How could he be so mild and serene with the Terrible One looking at him like that?

Then Thaxmosis did something he had never done before, or at least Jura could not remember him doing it. The Terrible One raised an eyebrow and whispered with stunned words as if he were alone. "No, that is improbable. None would have crossed into the Endless Waste..."

"Palaxnym said the very same my lord, and then he remembered the tome by Cenloth. The historian he said had written about the night Pallator fell and he recorded the names of some who escaped. Palaxnym thought he could confirm the names he heard with any reference Cenloth had penned."

"Go with Jura and do as she says. Do not think of returning to see Palaxnym or Ith young one, both are beyond any help you could give them." Thaxmosis whispered quickly spinning and leaving the cavern in a sudden rush.

"Where is he going?" Voarothim asked a silent Jura and it

took a moment for her to answer after she exhaled her held breath.

"To his chamber maybe, or to his hoard down deeper in the caves. It is where he goes when he needs to think. Why are you asking?" Jura inquired when she saw the manner at which he watched the old one leave. This was part of a plan Jura instantly realized as the Red Dragon approached her.

"Then the work area where he created the poison, it will be unguarded?"

"You cannot go there," Jura replied so hastily she had to stop and gather herself, "I mean Thaxmosis will not be there but there are others. We cannot go freely through his lair. It is not allowed and someone will tell him."

Voarothim shook his head and whispered, "Tell me where Thaxmosis makes the potions."

"No, we are not allowed there. Why do you wish to know of that place when we cannot help Palaxnym and Ith?" Jura responded trying to make the Wyrm understand his new and permanent situation. Yes, it was deplorable this life at time, but after a few years it would be acceptable.

"Because I know-

"No, he will discover what you have done, where you have gone!"

"How to save Palaxnym and Ith-"

"He will punish you, us both, for not obeying his command!" Jura hissed angrily, her patience finally done with this new comer. Why did he not understand, see with his eyes what his circumstances were now.

"I cannot leave my family to die Jura. I will not do that, so tell me where the work area is or I will search for it myself." Voarothim calmly, just like before, replied while staring deeply into her eyes.

And there it was, one last time. The calm and serene feelings that came from those dark eyes pulled at her pushing the fear she had for Thaxmosis and his...punishments away. Could she chance an escape again?

Three

Stunk was not your typical Ogre by any stretch of the imagination. He was rather normal as it goes for the appearance of an Ogre by the race standards, in that he had two thick legs, two long muscular arms, and a head which may or may not have been too large for his shoulders. He had dull grey skin, stringy and oily long hair in which twigs and leaves and berries from an array of fauna had become entangled. He was not a very bright Ogre if you asked his father Stank, which is why the non-typical Ogre drew guard duty outside of the cave entrance...during the daylight. It was not a mystery that most, if not all, Ogres hated the light, shunned the glowing rays of the fire orb in the sky, all but Stunk that is. He really kind of liked being out during the day and seeing all the life of the swamp around the cave. He smiled dully at the butterflies and the birds which glided by, even giggled as the animals and insects fled from him in pure terror. As a matter of fact, everything fled from poor Stunk when he approached it. He never realized, even thought, an eight-foot grey giant with big black eyes, stringy black hair, and a few warts growing here and there might be scary.

"What in the white wind of the North are you doing?"

Stunk turned his attention from looking around the fabulous world outside the cave back to the small human standing at his side. His name was Torg and Stunk hated him so, well, not really. Stunk really could never bring himself to hate if you wanted to know. Torg used to be an Odi, one of the Northmen of the Endless Waste who lived in clans and killed anything that was not Odi. Stunk even heard the Odi killed Trolls and Ogres and ate them, yes, ate them!

"I was looking at everything," Stunk remarked pointing out into the swamp.

"Why, is it not the same swamp it was yesterday and the day before that one, and the day before that one?" Torg spat as his hand squeezed the handle of a very large mace.

"Oh no," Stunk came back with a bright smile showing off teeth which were greener than a Troll's skin, "there are some new flowers over there and-"

"Flowers?" Torg asked in shock.

"-and a nest of squirrels-"

"Just what kind of Ogre are you?" Torg spat again, the

exasperation in his voice easily sensed.

The question stopped Stunk in his happy description of all the new things he had found this afternoon in the swamp. He cocked his head to the right and looked just a little lost as he answered. "Well...I do not know. Are there other kinds of Ogres?"

"No, there is no other Ogre like you Stunk I have ever seen, and if there is I hope it dies before being called by the Dark One. One of you here at the Lair is all I can take."

Oh, now that hurt Stunk thought as he brought his rather large head back to a straight upright spot on his neck. "Why would you wish for an Ogre to die?"

"Listen, you stay right here, understand?" Torg snapped pointing to the ground at Stunk's feet. The Ogre only nodded still confused as to what was happening as Torg shook his head. "Good, I am going over there."

As the Northman walked away Stunk was still lost as to why and he called out, "why are you going over there?"

"To get away from you before whatever it is that makes you like you gets on me."

Oh, Stunk thought, all right. The Ogre had missed the

painful malice of the remark, or maybe he did and he was used to such things of this world. Whatever it was Stunk just turned and went back to looking out on the swamp with a happy eye.

"Am I truly seeing this, an Odi and an Ogre both guard the entrance to the cave?"

Baldric took a moment to state the obvious answer to the question, which he knew would only bring about a second question he already knew. "Yes, it is an Odi and an Ogre standing watch."

"Now why would two bitter enemies like an Odi and an Ogre stand watch instead of killing each other?" Lalya whispered, the question dripping with derision. She barely held her disdain in check Rehema thought as she watched the pair by the cave entrance. Lalya was at least trying to play nice.

"I do not know why the pair refuses to kill each other, but I am sure it is not due to the influence of an Ancient Dragon, as you are assuming." Baldric sneered shaking his head. He looked to the brothers giving them a silent signal with his eyes and both replied in kind gesturing they understood. The thief need his people thinking the same before entering the cave while behind the Anthros were a little lost.

"This does not feel right, not in the least. Something or someone has gathered and influenced Mythical Ones to guard them." Lalya stated looking to Rehema and then Elas. Both the Daes only looked back quietly choosing not to speak. The Fox knew both were thinking the same, there was no choice but to enter the cave and face whatever was there. Lalya understood this as well, freeing Sefu was the only choice there was now. She gave a grumble and checked her twin hand held crossbows as Baldric spoke up.

"We will take the Odi, you Anthros can take the-"

Before the thief could finish his words the Ogre suddenly began to move, leaving his post and wandering into the swamp. Elas pulled the small sword from the scabbard on his back and smiled, his maw pulling back to show his sharp canines. "Luck shines on us. Let us make entry quick before the Ogre returns."

Well, that was not helpful Baldric thought as he only nodded to the Dea's command. The thief had hoped to at least weaken the three Anthros by having them take the Ogre, but that was not going to happen now. Baldric bit his bottom lip in frustration and moved out in silence with the others keeping low using the brush and vegetation to hide his approach. The six thieves made no sound and barely stirred the environment as they passed leaving Torg the Odi unawares until the very last moment. He was standing by the entrance still frustrated and angry about that fool of an Ogre when six bodies came out of the swamp like ghosts, the setting sun hiding them. He jerked reaching for the mace on his hip just as a human threw a knife with a snap of his arm. There was a sudden sting in Torg's upper shoulder as the blade struck and buried itself to the hilt, but the pain was nothing to Torg. He was Odi. His skin was thick and tough. He turned to raise the alarm by pulling the cord which would sound the bells below; only just as he did he felt his body literally explode in agony. With a blink he fell to the ground convulsing uncontrollably as foam began to fly from his mouth. He took one last gurgling breath as the ghosts slipped past and into the mouth of the cave unseen by anyone else.

As the thieves came to a stop in the dark shadows thrown by the walls of the tunnel Lalya hissed to Rolft, "was your blade covered in poison?"

"What if it is? We leave none behind to talk."

The Fox growled and began to raise the hand holding her small crossbow. It looked as if the party's solidarity had finally come to the end of the road when Elas suddenly appeared between Lalya and the human. "Sefu...we are here for our brother larcener," he spoke quickly and low bringing the possible altercation to an end.

"When this is done..." Lalya whispered back as the Dae ushered her down the tunnel, farther into the cavern.

Rolft only watched the Anthros silently shuffle away smiling wickedly. Yes, little fox, when this is done there will be a reckoning and you will be the first to fall.

A bush down the worn trail had suddenly shook, rattled just a bit, and the movement caught Stunk's observant eye making him smile. Then the sound, which was next, took a moment to register to Stunk and he realized with a bigger smile that the squirrels must have come back. Oh Stunk so wanted a pet, so very much, and a little squirrel would be perfect. He could pet the squirrel and love him and pet him and love him and-

The bush shook again, just a little louder and a little longer this time.

Stunk was still thinking about his new pet squirrel and how he'd pet him and love him and pet him and call him Stink. He was so deep and seduced by the vision of his new friend Stunk actually stopped on the trail and stood perfectly still in its middle while looking off in space with a happy expression.

A heavy sigh sounded, loud enough that it should have attracted some attention. It did not though so this time the bush shook so hard it almost tore its roots free and it still barely caught Stunk's attention. Yet it did and the Ogre bent quickly at the waist at the sound, so fast in fact there was a sudden ripping sound that one might suspect, could have easily assumed was a torn loin cloth…that's if Stunk wore one, which he did because the small kilt like cloth was perfect for him he thought. The Ogre slowly crept, plodded with such heavy steps the ground shook just a bit, up on the bush. He shushed a bird that was overhead loudly chirping for no reason…except that it might be scared. And when Stunk was close enough he put his club down by the trunk of a tree and reached out slowly, oh so slow, to part the leaves of the bush and get a glimpse of his new pet squirrel.

Yet, when the leaves parted, there was no squirrel. There was nothing there but more leaves and more branches and no pet. Stunk frowned sadly showing his large yellow and green teeth before stepping back from the noisy bush visibly upset. He truly wanted a pet squirrel his small brain thought as he reached down to take up his club again, only the large hunk of branch was no longer there. Now who took my club Stunk started to think staring at the ground where his weapon had just been then turning to look behind him? As the Ogre did he came close to catching sight of his club, that large wooden branch, as it crashed down onto his head with a loud crack. Stunk gave a grunt as the club broke in half then he quickly stiffened and fell face first into the bushes he had been searching through for his new pet squirrel.

Jared stepped back noting the Ogre was still breathing which made him happy. He tossed the broken half of the club into the bushes to hide it as well, the need for the branch through after knocking out the Ogre. Jared took a quick look left then right before moving out toward the cave entrance to catch up with the humans and Anthros. They were his cover for getting past the other guards and protectors. He moved quick and silent, the worn boots and canvas pants making no sound as he trotted to the cave, the rusted small sword strapped on his side held in place by his hand keeping it quiet. His tall lean frame meshed with the plants and fauna right up to the opening and then Jared froze at the sight of the body lying out in the open. He took two long careful steps approaching the human slowly. Jared could see the dagger sticking of the human's chest and the foam dripping from the man's blue lips. He leaned in and took a sniff of the oozing yellow bubbles then jerked his nose away.

Poison...they killed the human in the worst way possible, no honor or chance for survival. Jared slipped back away from the body wondering whose blade had done the evil deed, was it one of the Anthros or a human? Whoever had done this, whichever group, someone was more than ready to kill. Whoever did this could easily do it again. Jared felt better now for leaving the Ogre alive in the bushes and held onto that feeling as he moved into the caves. The dark slowed him for a moment as his eyes adjusted to the change but then another change caught Jared unprepared.

The dirt and rocky floor of the tunnel suddenly changed under his boots. It went from what he had expected and had been traversing to a smooth, hand worked surface. Jared stopped and knelt running the flat of his palm over the floor, which is what the ground had turned into, and felt small cuts and grooves in the stone. Patterns were carved into small block just over a hand length long and two wide, lines were created as the block buttressed up against another and then another. He looked to his right noting the wall was starting to transform from a rough gritty facade to the same smooth hand carved stone. Jared rose to his full seven-foot height and looked at the ceiling overhead...it was the same as the floor and walls. This Thaxmosis, it had turned the cave into something more hospitable for everyday life he assumed.

He had hoped to follow the tracks of the humans and

Anthros, but the chance to do such a thing was gone. The stones he walked on were free of dirt or dust; almost freshly swept it looked like. Jared crouched and began to move forward again, quietly and with caution hoping if he were lucky he would catch the group. The slope of the tunnel changed, steepened, as he traveled deeper into the complex. How far down does this cave go? Jared thought as the light from outside faded more with each step he took. It was getting dark, maybe too much so he thought more as the swamp and its light disappeared being replaced by the low light of torches burning in sconces along the wall. The tunnel ran downward, the angle of descent steepening more, and then the corridor leveled and came to a fork running into two separate halls made of the same stone. Jared stopped again, looked down the first new hall and then down the other. There were no footprints to follow down either, no way to know which one of the halls the others took. No way to tell which one would take him to Thaxmosis and which one would lead him to where ever. Well, Jared thought, I'll just have to guess and hope for the best.

It took just a moment, a beat of a calm heart, for the choice to be made. Jared crouched again and began to head down the right hall hoping he would find the others in a moment or two. The hall was lit with torches just like the first one and the yellow light gave no assistance in telling if someone had walked down this passage recently. The illumination was barely enough for Jared to see a few lengths of his arm in front of his face which made it seem as if the corridor ran on forever. He took careful steps slipping down the hall quietly till out of the dark he saw on the west wall the opening for a new passage. Jared began to smile, a new route and a new chance to find the others.

Then his foot snagged on something, an invisible wire running just an ankle height from one wall to the other. He heard the snap of the wire as he stepped forward fully, the loud clank of gears springing in sudden action next, and then the floor dropping completely out from under his feet. Jared felt his body go weightless just as a long arm sprang free from the wall he was standing close to. It is a trap his mind screamed as he began to fall, he had stepped right into a trap. The bar swung at him so fast Jared barely had time to see the long spikes that had popped out along its spine, only felt the sting as the barb punctured the side of his hand where he stopped the arm before it could hit him. Then the dark of the shaft he was disappearing into took over and Jared was free falling downward into the unknown.

Rehema heard the snap of the trip wire from the hall and quickly looked around the corner from the new corridor on the west wall where she was hiding. She caught a fleeting glimpse of the one who had set off the trap, watched him fall into the shaft of the pit that opened beneath him. From behind her Lalya stepped out into the hall just enough to see while whispering. "Was it the one who was following us?"

"It had to be, the guards know where the traps are Lalya." Elas grumbled as he stepped completely out into the hall. Unlike his friends the Canine was not worried about being seen for the moment.

The Serval though paid little attention to either, her tail twitching nervously from side to side. She quickly trotted over to look down the shaft noting it only took up half the passage. The bar on the other hand, it went all the way across and the spines which protruded were covered with something. Elas walked up and sniffed the spike before looking to Rehema with a shake of his head, his tail freezing with abruptly.

"It is covered with something, maybe a concoction to knock one out."

"Then whoever fell down the shaft might be alive somewhere below?" Lalya asked as she walked up to see the pit.

"He could be a few lengths down the shaft or a halfway to the center of the swamp. Someone built the pit to remove a trespasser and do it quickly." Rehema whispered looking to where the arm had come to a stop. It was meant to stop a pair side-by-side, the first victim would fall to a fate unknown and the unfortunate one next to them would be pierced and put to sleep, why? The question ran through Rehema's mind echoing with a loud wail as it did.

"It was a 'he'? Was 'he' Anthro or Human?" Lalya asked.

"He was...every race I know of." Rehema whispered in return to the question and when the confused look on her friend's face appeared the Cat talked on. "He was tall, like the Horses of the Plains and wide like an Ursi and he had our ears and a Simian's face."

Elas looked down the pit for a moment then back to Rehema, "how is that possible? No race looks like that, all of us as one, except..."

"The old tales of Pallator..." Lalya whispered adding her shock to the groups.

Rehema was about to agree with her friend, which is why she was confused about the one who followed, when the answer for the question from before of why a trap would put one of the pair to sleep abruptly popped into her mind. The confusion of seeing the one following them had slowed her instincts and now they were all in danger. "We have to leave! The guards will be coming to see who triggered the trap."

Lalya and Elas only nodded and moved with their friend as she took to a run fleeing the area in a flash. They ran down the new corridor and found Baldric and the brothers waiting for them halfway in. As the Serval came to a stop by the human he growled low. "That trap must have set off all kinds of alarms below. We have guards moving in."

"We will just have to be very quiet from here on in then." Rehema smiled and slipped past the human who looked at her stunned. She had no intention of leaving the lair without the gem. She had no intention what-so-ever of leaving her brother with Kazmir it seemed.

They were really going to go ahead with this, with the guards alerted now? As Elas went past Baldric just shook his head, crazed Anthros.

How far he fell down the pit Jared was not sure? The cramp quarters of the shaft made it easy for his long legs to push out forcing his body into a wedge and thus stopping his fall. His hand burned where it grabbed the bar and when Jared sniffed the strange gel by the cut the spike made his nose wrinkled. This was not some poison Jared's sense of smell told him, but whatever the liquid was supposed to do it had not...yet. He felt anger bite into his heart as he silently cursed himself for setting off the pitfall. After a moment, and a deep breath, Jared brought the anger under control. The problem now was which way to go to get out, up back to the hall or down to wherever the shaft led. Jared had no intention of dropping farther into the shaft, what if it ended with a bottom full of spears and spikes? No, the best choice was to go back up. And when he heard the voices talking above Jared felt a small sense of relief. It had to be the Anthros and look at that, he chose the right hall to follow them. Now that is lucky he thought with a smile, but then one of them mentioned guards coming, alerted by the activation of the trap, and the voices disappeared with a wisp of wind. No, the Anthros are leaving. Jared felt a twinge of panic and he started to inch his way back up the shaft. He had to keep the others in sight.

Then as he finished with another slide up the walls of the pit Jared heard someone approaching. Instinctively he stopped and held perfectly still as the voices overhead started to talk. He knew someone was looking down into the shaft as they spoke. Hopefully they will not see me down here hanging like a piece of meat Jared thought.

"You see anything down there?" The Odi Wik asked with a snap while looking down the open pit. It took just a moment or two for Rasch and Wik to make it to the trap after the alarms were raised down in the halls below. It was more than a little confusing and frustrating to find nothing by the prickly arm which is why he was a little testy.

"No," Rasch stated moving his head around trying to get a better glimpse down in the dark of the pit, "but if anyone went down the pit then they are meat for the Howler."

"Yea, but why is there not a body up here as well, sleeping away like it was night time." Wik retorted still confused.

"Probably just the one who came looking for loot and found death in its stead." Rasch answered turning to look at Wik with a frown.

The Odi looked to the empty spot on the floor where there should have been someone else before turning back to his fellow guard, "Yea, but there has always been one other when the trap is sprung."

"I know that, but this time there is only the one. Now, if we run, we can watch the Howler eat whoever fell down the pit."

Rasch smiled and headed off quickly down the hall.

Wik stood staring at the trap, at its sprung state, and wondered quietly why there was not a second body. There was always a second body for as long as he could remember, a body just sleeping away like it was nighttime. The Odi stood there for a moment longer when his fellow guard yelled for him and he had no choice but to follow. Still, where was the second body he thought as he ran to catch up?

The Howler, what was that? Jared sighed and shook his head, he came looking for a Thaxmosis and he almost had to meet up with a Howler. He looked up to the top of the pit and thought about squirming and inching his way back up there like some worm. Then Jared looked down into the dark of the pit and thought about what the men had said. The trap had set off alarms below, the men came from below and this Howler was below, so logic would seem to point to the obvious fact that Thaxmosis was more than likely below. With a low whisper Jared sighed and started to slide down the shaft.

"I guess I go down and meet this Howler face to face."

Four

Thaxmosis entered the massive chamber where he kept his hoard with long nervous strides. Any other time he would have stopped and enjoyed the sight of all the gleaming gold coins and sparkling gems, but this was no ordinary time. Thaxmosis had spent his considerably long life building and expanding his hoard of gold and rare items at the inconsequential cost of both Anthro and Human life...at least to him. The Dragon walked past pile after pile, some tall enough to almost touch the ceiling high overhead and some small, of gold and silver coin without even a glance so engrossed was he in thought. He passed a rack made of metal which held several longswords, short swords, and even axes and hammers which was nothing unique except for the fact every weapon possessed some small glow in the low light of the large chamber. Again, Thaxmosis paid no attention to his possessions as his mind turned over the information Voarothim had told him.

He walked on passing more piles and more racks till he was deep into his hoard among the rarest of items and the largest piles of coin and bars of precious metal. It was here, in the heart of all that he had taken and obtained that Thaxmosis felt at ease enough to begin to dissect what he thinking.

"They are gone, all the Paracletus, save for the few who survived that night and those are hidden from the world." Thaxmosis hissed in a dark whisper, the tendrils of bone hanging down from his chin moving with each word.

The Paracletus, magical warriors born and bred to be the protectors of the people of the Lands, were lost to the fogs of time now. During the Cataclysm the war between the five races of Anthros which formed the Great Society and the three races of Troll and Ogre and Giant which formed the hateful legion of Mythical Ones raged across the lands. The humans it seemed could not fully choose a side with most allying with the Society while the rest joining the monsters of the Mythical Ones. Even with the humans help though the Anthros were no match for a combined might of the ones from the North and when all seemed lost for the Society they came, the Paracletus, an army of men and women not of one race of Anthros, but a weave of all the races themselves. Thaxmosis had watched the battles between the Society and the Mythical and with an evil smile noted the combination of Northman and Troll, of Ogre and Giant was close to routing the poor Anthro and Human armies. Darkness, once it has tasted blood, will only seek greater destruction Thaxmosis thought. The Mythical Ones had driven the Anthros across the Plains where the Equines lived, driven the Ursi and the Burrowers deep inside their mountain cities to die behind barred gates and doors. The Simians and the Daes had taken to the trees and jungles of the immense forest of the South and East to make one last stand for life.

"And then they came, like a plague the Paracletus came."

Oh yes, like a divine light from the center of the lands the 'Protectors' came and with them death to the vast hordes of the monsters. Their number was small, not even a quarter of the Mythical Ones armies, and yet the Paracletus could not be stopped. They were superior warriors these new arrivals, magically altered or somehow enhanced, and with this power the 'Protectors' struck the Legion like a hammer thrown from the heavens. The Northman and Troll, the Ogre and Giant, all fell to the lesser numbers of the Paracletus, like wheat before the scythe. At the lead of these avengers and defenders of a new faith, at the very tip of the spear was the Dominum Summum, the Lord Supreme of the Paracletus, Marallel the First. In no time the 'Protectors' had pushed the monsters out of the mountains freeing the Ursi and the Mustelidae and then crushed the armies on the plains scattering the Mythical Ones to the winds like leaves. When the forces of the Simians heard of the change in the tide of the war the apes were emboldened, empowered and they fought back with a bravery only equaled by the Daes beside them, the Cats and Canines and Apes striking out and driving the Legion out of the South lands...with the help of their protectors of course.

"No one could match the Paracletus, no one could defeat them."

And with the end of the First Cataclysm, with what was left of the monsters fleeing over the Blood Peaks and Forlorn Mountains and into the Endless Waste, peace was the Society's reward. There was prosperity finally after so much desolation. There was life after too many deaths. There were protectors of this new peace too, the Paracletus, who pledged their strength of arms and courage of heart to keep the evil of the North away from the Society and its people. The grand castle of Pallator was erected as a symbol of the harmony of this new age, like a cathedral dedicated to the perseverance of the Great Society. The Five Races of the Society in turn pledged their devotion and allegiance to their protectors, sending offerings of wealth and individuals to live with the Paracletus. For a three hundred years the Society knew what it was to be looked after, the warmth of the blanket of being guarded.

"All things must come to an end though and such was the Paracletus reign..."

It has been eighty years since the night when the protectors of the Great Society fought each other to an ultimate stalemate, those loyal to Gareth the Lord Supreme of the time fighting those faithful to his Second, the Vicegerent Hirall Thaxmosis thought. No one truly knows why they fought each other to the death this Order devoted to protecting the Society, tales and speculation are the only words which have come from the ruins of Pallator these last years. Some say Gareth fell under the evil shadow of a spirit locked away in a rare longsword presented to the Summum as a gift from the Anthros. It was this nefarious spirit which made the accusations toward the Society, bloody threats of ending the reign of the ones who led each Race. Others say it was a simple and yet overpowering emotion that brought about the fall of the greatest warriors of the Lands, jealousy. Hirall wanted what Gareth had, his title and power and especially his companion, the fiercely beautiful Bryndul. The only truth that has ever come from that night was presented by the armies of the Society, the five races arriving as the castle burned brightly. The armies found no one alive, not a Paracletus or one the many followers in the burned out husk of the castle, or so they have told everyone since that fateful night. Rumors, whispers, though tell differently, that a few of the fabled warriors lived and are now hidden away in secret by the Anthros themselves. More importantly though, no one found all the gold and treasure the Paracletus were rumored to hold. No word as to where all the wealth given as offerings and tokens was now.

"So much gold...more than any Anthros or Human could imagine..."

At the end of his low exhale the image in his mind of so much gold that the piles could literally lay cramped against the ceiling of this huge cavern made Thaxmosis growl with lust. He was close to being Ancient, close to being so old that only an endless amount of treasure would show the proper respect he had earned with his long life, and the riches the Paracletus had acquired before leaving this realm would be just the amount needed. Thaxmosis smiled for a moment, a grin so evil had anyone who would have had the misfortune of catching a glimpse would surely feel their skin chill and their muscles shiver uncontrollably.

"So two have survived and both are in the Endless Waste...but how? More to the point, would they know where the riches of their Order were hidden?"

There was the crux of his predicament, one might say, the inevitable answer that would come of the pursuit of the gold. He would have to chance a journey outside of his lair, among the wilds of the Lands, to reach this pair. This could bring hated attention to his presence, a Dragon sighting these days would most certainly bring hunters and brigands. The risk of his demise was low, almost indeterminable at the hands of an Anthros or Human, but what if these Paracletus had no clue where the gold was taken. Should he risk the scrutiny of venturing outside, even for the gold? Thaxmosis chuckled, the sound akin to grating metal on metal.

"Silly question...of course it is worth the scrutiny...this is gold we are talking about."

The moment of levity, as cruel as it sounded, came to a quick end as one of the Troll Shaman's edged into Thaxmosis presence, slowly and carefully. The Shaman was no fool. He had seen his master rip others, Ogre and Northman alike, to pieces for simply disturbing him as he walked along the halls. He called to the old one with a tremble in his high pitched voice. "Ma...master."

"What," Thaxmosis spat and sighing with anger at the same moment, distractions, always with the distractions.

The Troll jumped a little and then spoke quickly, "we have intruders master."

"More intruders, are there other Dragons?"

"We are not sure Master," The Shaman shook his head sending the many rings through his large ears jingling, "the trap was sprung at the entrance and the guards are going to check."

Thaxmosis turned to his follower, more like a slave really, and eyed the green being with a hard eye. The Shaman was just a foot shorter than Thaxmosis, maybe more now that the Troll was slinking away from his gaze. Dominance, it was the way of the Wyrms. It was true that Trolls regenerated, cuts healing at a rapid rate while severed limbs could return in a day, which made them formidable and dangerous foes. Yet the Dragon also knew there was no coming back from the acid he spits, the skin and bone melting from the viscous liquid in moments. Dominance...it was the rule by which all followed, either voluntarily or involuntarily.

"Bring me word when you know what it was that set off the traps, until then double the guards and the rovers. If there is an intruder loose in my home, I want it dealt with quickly." He ordered and the Troll quickly agreed to with a vigorous nod of its head. The Shaman left the cavern with quick steps obviously happy to be free of his master's bearing. Thaxmosis watched the Shaman leave then turned his attention back to the task at hand, how to retrieve the gold of the Paracletus? His nemesis Palaxnym had come looking for the tome written by the historian Cenloth. He had not read the tome himself, only wished to have it among the many works in his library. He had been told the Weasel was mundane with his prose and far too odd to be taken seriously, and yet the book just may be the key to the lock he was trying to open. The smile from before, the malevolence it oozed, came back as the Dragon began to stroke the tendrils on his chin.

They walked along the halls quickly, one's head bowed to keep from making eye contact with any passerby while the other looked around in an endless and unhidden fascination. Voarothim barely had time to examine his surroundings until now and with this sudden chance he took as hard and as scrutinizing a look as he could while walking. Before coming to the den of 'Thaxmosis the Terrible', Voarothim wondered if one day he would have such a silly moniker placed at the end of his name, Palaxnym had described what to expect once inside the cave. What the Gold Dragon had described though matched very little from what the young Dragon's eyes took in. The walls and ceiling of the Old One's lair were carved stone put in careful place by hands and not hard rock chiseled by underwater rivers and streams. The young Dragon wondered just how long it took Thaxmosis to have the elaborate work done. The transformation of the caves into a sanctuary must have taken ages he thought silently as he walked along. Then Voarothim's eyes spotted two large Trolls moving along the hall quickly toward them, the beady eyes of the pair of large green beings lingering on the pair of Wyrms for just a moment before both were past them.

"Where do his followers come from?" Voarothim asked turning back to Jura who he was following.

She had been silent this whole time, not out of the necessity to hide though that was high on the list of things Jura was keeping in mind. No, she had been quiet out of the feeling of dread. After leaving the chamber where Palaxnym and Ith were being kept in the magical space both Dragons had made a quick heading toward the chamber where Thaxmosis worked with his Alchemy, yet just after a few steps Voarothim made a quick change to the plan. Now he needed to visit the Terrible One's library to retrieve a tome from the collection before going to get the antidote for the poison which was sending Palaxnym and Ith into a forever-sleep. Jura had barely begun to fight this addendum to what was already a crazed plan, which she was still not sure why she was having any part of, when the young Dragon just shook his head and walked by. Voarothim intended to find both the library and the laboratory, with or without her. He was a fool, courageous and unshakable from his need to save Palaxnym and Ith, but a fool nonetheless because he refused to see where he was Jura thought. No one defied Thaxmosis, those who had made such a decision felt more than any description of the worst agony, and here he was asking about followers.

And here she was answering him, "they are drawn here...to him."

"Drawn here?"

"Yes," Jura whispered looking up from the floor just enough to keep her bearings in the hall, "the same as those with a good heart are drawn to Palaxnym those with a dark heart are drawn to Thaxmosis."

"So, the Trolls and Northman, they come here from as far as the Endless Waste to join with the Old One?" Voarothim asked quickly, his curiosity brimming now.

Jura sighed heavily with frustration, why he cannot see the danger in this she could not comprehend. "No, they come because the dark in their hearts pulls at them, tells them to come here. Once here Thaxmosis uses his 'influence' to corrupt their weak minds and wills, bends the poor souls to his beck and call."

"His 'influence', is it like a magical spell of some kind?"

This was it, the end of this idea of...whatever they were doing Jura thought angrily as she came to an abrupt stop in the hall. No longer did she bow her head to hide her yellow eyes which glowed with anger as she stared hard the Red Dragon. "We go no farther with this!"

Voarothim almost bumped into Jura coming to a stop just a breath away from her, the nose on his face almost touching her nose. His eyebrow arched a little as he questioned this sudden pause, "what, we have to stop talking?"

"No," Jura snapped shaking her head while holding up one green hued hand, the small scales on the back running up to her nails, "this absurd idea in which we save Palaxnym and Ith. There is no disobeying Thaxmosis and there is no saving Palaxnym from his fate!"

The raised eyebrow lowered slowly as understanding slowly graced Voarothim. He shook his head just as slow and whispered calmly so as not press Jura farther in her state. "I am going to help Palaxnym and Ith. There is no persuading me otherwise."

"No, there is no persuading you, is there? If you knew Voarothim, what will happen to us when we are caught then you would say differently, that I am sure of." Jura replied coldly, or maybe it was fear.

Voarothim was young and still learning his way with

others. Was this response anger or was it based on something deeper, a fear born of treatment? He was a Dragon, hidden away from the races lest he face an uncertain fate, so his interactions with others had been limited and protected by Palaxnym and Ith. He took a breath and gambled with his life as well as that of his guardians. "You are not the wyrmling of Thaxmosis, are you Jura?"

The question froze the very breath of the young Green Dragon, the air on her insides freezing her bones. Voarothim saw this, could easily see it on her face, and it was somewhat expected so he pressed. "I am not the wyrmling of Palaxnym and Ith either. They found me in the cold of the mountains of the North, so young I have no memories of that day or before. Both took me in, Ith nursing me and raising me with Palaxnym becoming my sire in my mind. I cannot leave them to die in an endless sleep Jura. I will not let a cruel fate such as that befall either of them."

The pair stood quietly in the hall staring at each other. Voarothim kept his dark eyes locked to the bright yellow of Jura's hoping she could see the resolve there, the intention of not letting his guardians suffer or pass from this world, and Jura never wavered with her eyes from his, those dark orange orbs full of strength. She sighed knowing now she would never escape this insane plan and spoke low, "What is this tome you need? Is it the one from Cenloth?"

"No, the Cenloth request was a ruse Palaxnym told me to say if Thaxmosis were to capture us."

The Green Dragon blinked and leaned in, "A ruse...a ruse for what?"

"We need to go," Voarothim stated and nodded down the hall and it was only then Jura noticed more and more of the denizens of the lair were walking by, "something is stirring the guards and others."

She turned and began to walk leading the Red Dragon toward the library of the Terrible One, his precious treasury of written works. As she did Jura looked back whispering, "Are you telling me this incursion was a plan? Palaxnym and Ith 'planned' on getting caught?"

"Yes, in a manner of speaking. Palaxnym knew Thaxmosis would never let him see the tome he required and he also knew the Terrible One would never pass on...'possessing' a true Red Dragon, one of the last of our kind. So he told me there would be a moment when I was free of the harsh eyes of the Terrible One and when the time came I was too find the tome and free us from Thaxmosis. He told me to say 'Paracletus' and the mention of the word would send the Terrible One following a blind trail."

Voarothim answered.

There are no more Red Dragons left in the Lands? Jura was not sure how to respond, once more the words from Voarothim leaving her speechless. The Gold Dragon had taken a risk of unimaginable consequence placing all of his faith in a young Wyrm to free him, only now it had become 'save' and not 'free'. A race against time to save his life and Ith's, now that was something Palaxnym had not planned for Jura thought as she picked up the pace of her walk. Thaxmosis surely would have gone to be with his hoard of gold and treasure, a place which induced clear thought for him, and that meant the library would be empty...hopefully Jura thought.

It just twitched...again.

The Odi Kess stopped in his run to the upper level when the movement of a small yellow worm just at the edge of the corner of the hall up ahead caught his eye. It looked like the end of a cat's tail, but then the thing disappeared out of sight. Kess cocked his to the right and stared at the junction for a long moment hesitant to move because he was not truly positive on what he had just seen. Was it a worm or was it the end of a cat's tail? He could not convince himself of either due to the short glance he saw of the thing, and then suddenly it appeared again, just as quick with a snap before disappearing.

"What are you little thing?" Kess whispered as he walked cautiously toward the corner to see what he had come across, only the Northman had no chance to discover what it was that captured his attention. No matter how cautious he had been poor Kess simply was not prepared for what happened next. As he reached the corner and peered round the wall a large pair of Anthro hands grabbed the side of his head and the last thing Kess saw was a Canine face coming out of the shadows and speeding toward his brow. When the blow struck it was more than enough to subdue him, rendering him unconscious with ease.

Rehema watched as Elas drug the limp Northman into the shadows. The thief would quickly hide the human and more importantly leave him alive. As the group waited Baldric edged out and looked down the hall, both ways, before leaning back in to speak. "Is it wise to leave him alive?"

"A sleeping body only raises suspicions sometimes while a dead one raises an alarm all the time." The Serval Cat replied back before leaning out to take her own look at hall.

We are in too deep for this job she thought taking a sniff of the air to scent it. Being followed by someone into the caves of what might be the lair for a very old Dragon was enough of an absurd challenge, but now that the trap had been sprung upstairs the halls were filling quickly with guards. Oh, and in addition to that, they were lost. The group barely found the hidden door to this level and that was not a good sign. Scars had instructed the group before leaving Thesedell there was a chamber deep in the caves which was filled with treasure, untold amounts of gold from ground to ceiling, praise be, and all he wanted from this place of splendor was a single large diamond gem. Bring me this gem, he had whispered with a cold intent to Rehema, bring the diamond back to me and Sefu will be freed. Well, as usual when dealing with the Rat, the details were lost in the vision of all the gold. Kazmir had failed to mention there were halls, actual stone carved blocks, and there were levels to this 'cave'. So, here were six thieves divided by mistrust along racial lines deep inside the lair of a Dragon with no idea of where to go. Yes, that about sums up this disaster of a job Rehema thought as she leaned back in.

"The guards are too many for my liking." Lalya whispered looking back where they had come from before turning back to Rehema.

The Serval only nodded as one of the brothers, Rolft, whispered. "We need to force one of these guards to tell us where the treasure chamber is?"

"Well, your chance to do that is coming. Everyone hide!" Baldric growled and all six thieves slipped into the shadows becoming one with the dark. The young Northman came trotting down the hall in obvious distress. His attention was lax as he hurried to comply with the order of his master and reach the upper level, which aided in his capture. Just as he passed the junction he felt hands grab him a blink before he was violently yanked into the dark. So hard was he pulled that a dagger fell from his belt to the floor, but it did not set long. A Troll passing by saw the blade and bent to pick it up, not the finest knife the beast thought...just good enough to maybe pull meat from the bone. The Troll then continued on his way, tucking the knife in a pouch on his belt while moving through the hall searching for intruders as ordered.

Five

Its lower mandible jutted out past the upper by more than it should have. The nose of the thing was misshaped, bent and too large, yet not one breath flowed through the large openings of the nostrils. The left eye was too small for the oversized face and the right angled downward from the outside corner toward the cheek, as if the side of the thing's head had melted from some catastrophic accident. Its hands were turned backward, not from the wrist but higher up at the elbow, and the arms were stretched longer than normal, so far down the knuckles on the deformed hands drug the ground because its legs were far too short for its body.

The Howler was, used to be, an Ogre which had the cruel fate of being pulled by a stark unrelenting desire to the Thathu Swamp in the South, drawn there from its tribe and home in the North by the darkness in its large heart. It had come to the swamp not understanding why it did, only that here is where it should be, and when it arrived the Master took over. Thaxmosis had been waiting for a special subject, one he could pay special attention too, and when the Howler appeared the Terrible One put his new found taste for alchemy and magic to a horrific undertaking. The Dragon had experimented on and twisted the Ogre through its dark magic and malevolent will till there was no semblance of the old beast, just the woeful thing all called the Howler now. The Ogre had long forgotten its true name, lost in nights of unimaginable pain and agony, to where now there was just Howler, a name placed upon it by its handler because it could do nothing more than howl. So, placed in a cage where the end of the shaft from the pit on the upper level opened in the ceiling, the beast stood ready to consume its meal for the night. This was its life, or what it understood life was. When the bell on the wall rings food comes down out of the opening hitting the filthy stone floor with a great big gush.

Only nothing came out of the shaft as it was supposed to, no meal. The Howler stood ready to eat, its small warped mind doing what it had been taught by its handler and the man's whip. Sometimes it ate good did the Howler, but sometimes it did not eat. It stood waiting like a good beast by the end of the shaft looking up with its ruined eyes, a long purple tongue hanging outside of the corner of its mouth. It stood there staring up into the dark of the opening waiting patiently, something should have fallen through it broken mind told it. The bell rang on the wall like always, where was the food? The Howler turned and looked to the fat Northman who stood by the locked door to the cage. "Oooooo," it called out trying to communicate in the only way it knew how.

"To the dung beetles with this, someone should have fallen out by now!" The Northman hissed obviously upset at having to attend to the Terrible One's pet.

"Oooooo," the Howler cried nodding with its misshaped head up to the ceiling and the opening.

"I know you are hungry!"

"Oooooo," the Howler nodded to the opening again.

"To the dung beetles with you too!" The Northman growled while opening the cage door and charging in. He was not afraid of the beast, why when he was the one charged with ensuring it was attended too, and the small whip he gripped in his right hand was the tool he used most to ensure the Howler followed his orders. The Northman squeezed the handle of the scourge so tight the leather squeaked loudly and the noise had an instant impact. The Howler began to shake its head and back away to the corner of the cage seeking safety. It knew the sound too well. Its mind may have been broken but it knew what would happen now, the pain of being hit over and over by the small whip sending terror through its heart.

"OOOOO!" It wailed falling to the stone and sliding away.

"I am going to beat you to very steps of death and th-"

There was a sudden sound up by the ceiling, inside the shaft. The Northman ended his attempted torture of the Howler leaving the beast to cry on the floor as he looked up into the shaft to see what made the noise. Maybe who ever fell down the pit was hung up part way down? Then, before the human could react, the person in the shaft appeared. Well, it was the owner of the very large boot which the Northman saw the last moment he was alive. He did not feel the sole land squarely on his face or the sudden snap of his neck as the weight of the person added so much force to the blow the bones which supported his head broke clean through. The Northman knew nothing, felt nothing, except he was done with this world and his actions on it had doomed his soul to an eternity in a very dark place.

Jared had wedged his body inside the shaft, up far enough to keep the eyes of the beast below from seeing him. Then when it had fallen away and the Odi had appeared he decided it was time to get out this shaft. His legs burned from 'walking' down the shaft of the pit so the relief he felt when Jared finally let go of the walls was indescribable. As he fell he brought his legs under him, his knees to his chest, and when he was out of the shaft

Jared kicked driving the sole of his boot right into the human's face with a loud crunch. The blow took the Northman off his feet in an instant and Jared pressed down even more with his leg as he stood on the human's head, riding the Odi right down into the tiled floor. A second loud crunch echoed in the room where the cage was and then it was eerily silent for a moment as Jared stood triumphantly on what used to be despicable man.

"Ooooo," the Howler cried after a moment of looking to the new thing in its cage with its large eye. It was...friend...not food the thing decided as its long tongue's spilled from its mouth again, rolling out like a scroll.

"What have they done to you?" Jared whispered looking back at the thing after a moment, staring not with fear or anger but compassion. In the large single black eye he could see something; a feeling telling him there was nothing to be wary of from the beast. Maybe it was just a foolish notion Jared thought, his youth showing through, but the thing had yet to attack him. He took a small step backward sliding his foot off the head of the dead Northman and as he did the thing edged a little closer and made the garbled sound again.

"Ooooo,"

He stepped away from the body of the dead Odi again and as he did Jared blinked and spoke low to the thing. "You can leave now, escape to the outside...if you want."

Why did I say that, the last bit? The thought had barely crossed Jared's brain as the thing moved closer making the garbled sound again. I said it because I know it will not leave this place Jared thought taking another step back. This is home to it, the only one it knows...understands. I might even fail at dragging it out of here he thought one last as the thing took the last two steps up to the body, its mouth and tongue watering. Jared turned to leave out of the open door to the cage silently thanking his luck for not having to witness what was coming. He took note of the bones lying around the large cage and knew instantly supper had been served. As he stepped out of the cage sounds of approaching feet warned him to take the east passage as the west was occupied with guards. Jared never looked back as he disappeared down the passage.

He silently crept down the hall using the shadows to hide in, still wondering if the thing back in the cell would try and leave when Jared heard screaming and yelling from behind. He stopped and looked back from the safety of the dark. A roar, loud and full of warning, then erupted and Jared could picture what was occurring. The guards he had heard approaching obviously strayed too close to the thing's food and now the fight was on. There was more screaming, more pleading, and then all was quiet...too quiet Jared thought.

If it had not sought escape, Jared asked no one but his own mind, then maybe it had found peace. Whatever happened he was done with the beast nevertheless Jared told himself. It was time to find this Thaxmosis and be gone from this lair.

The sanctuary of his treasure chamber was little solace this night to Thaxmosis. His mind was still racing with how to put his clawed hands on all the gold the Paracletus had acquired over so many years then hid just before the end of their Order. He walked among the large piles of his treasure hoard thinking, his centuries of maturity and experiences all focused on one single point now, one object. How do I obtain all that gold?

He was buried deep in speculation using the depth of his logic to solve this dilemma when a sparkle caught his eye. It was from the small hammer shaped head of just that, a small hammer sitting on top of an antique pedestal, some piece of furniture the Dragon had obtained from somewhere in his past. Thaxmosis walked over to the weapon feeling a break in his thinking of the Paracletus gold was needed. As he stopped by the pedestal he looked carefully at the weapon on its perch. The first thing to catch one's eye was the fact the handle was far too big for such a small head of a hammer. The second were the inscriptions running up the sides of said handle; engravings which to this day were still a mystery to the Dragon. He reached out and took hold of the hammer and lifted it with ease. It was then one would note the handle was not made of wood like most axes and hammers, but of some dull metal that resembled timber.

"Why would someone make a handle to look like wood when it was not wood?" Thaxmosis whispered thinking to no one but himself.

The Dragon turned the weapon in its side holding it in his two hands. It was so light, hardly any weight to its bulk so it would be useless in a fight. It was four hands long from butt to the grip. Well...his hands were larger than a human. The head was the same dull metal as well and like any other hammer, both ends square with a small spike on the top. The Dragon sighed thinking, partially, about why he had even killed those Trolls for such a useless thing like this. Then his eyes fell on the inscriptions again and he remembered why he melted those Trolls down to goo and Thaxmosis smiled.

"Because you are a mystery and I will know all of your secrets one-day my little friend."

He placed the hammer back on the pedestal gently still

smiling before letting his eyes drift to the pair of weapons leaning against the pedestal, two very special swords. Thaxmosis had come across both recently. The first was a short sword, a single edged blade with a curved end, closely resembling the scimitars the Simian soldiers carry in the South forests. Only the Dragon knew this was no ordinary blade by any means, it smelled of magic, glowed with the sorcery used to create it. The other sword was the same, magically enhanced in some way, only it was longer than the first by two hands' and edged on both sides like a long sword. The pommels and handles of both were typical, shaped without the exceptional artistry one would most certainly take when forging a weapon to be imbued with magic. This, among the other hidden secrets, teased the Dragon with a silent cruelty just as the hammer did.

"And I will know your secrets as well, oh brothers in arms."

He stood there eyeing all three weapons with an evil gaze when he heard the clink of a gold coin being kicked. Thaxmosis took a small sniff and knew it was the Troll Shaman from before, coming to bring him news obviously. "What do we know?" He asked with a cold mood refusing to look or acknowledge the Troll's presence.

"The trap is empty Master." The Troll remarked with a rough grinding voice. It bowed its head and hesitated for a moment which instantly drew the full attention of the Dragon who snapped his gaze to the follower.

"What is that?" Thaxmosis growled and snarled.

The hesitation went on for another moment as the Troll refused to look up from the floor where his eyes were locked on a large tile stone. If he was going to die horribly, like so many others, then he preferred not to see it happen. "The guards on the upper floors...there was a Northman who had been rendered unconscious-"

"What are you saying fool? Spit It Out!"

"The intruders Master...the Northman we found...says...he thinks-" The Troll stammered now in full panic, images of being melted by the acidic breath of the Dragon filing his mind.

"The intruders are still FREE...In My HOME!" Thaxmosis spat and yelled.

Oh here it is. I'm going to be melted into a giant green puddle of goo, the Troll thought as it fought the panic trying to speak. "No Master...Yes I mean...the intruders are...we know one fell into the...I am sorry!"

Yet there was no attack, no acid melting skin and flesh and bone to a puddle. The Dragon only growled and pushed his way past his follower shoving the Troll aside with a hard bump of his body. Thaxmosis had every intention to kill, no torture, every single living thing, be it Anthro or human, which had made the poor decision to invade his lair. He moved swiftly, the bottom half of the long robes around his body flowing and snapping with the Dragon's quick steps. Thaxmosis then came to an even quicker stop when alarms began to shout and ring out from all corners of the vast underground dungeon. The Dragon turned to the Troll with a shocked expression before snarling, his upper lip twisting in fury.

"I want these intruders caught and brought to me so I can personally see to their demise."

The Troll only nodded and ran for the way to freedom from the gaze of the Terrible One, bolted past the Dragon and away from the treasure room. Thaxmosis watched as the Troll ran from him but his mind took none of the sight in. He was already thinking where he needed to be at the moment, where he thought this was all going to come to a head you might say. Palaxnym had come looking for a book, well, he brought along extra help it seems. The Dragon then left his hoard of gold and precious items without so much as a glance back. He was headed for his library, to catch the ones who had invaded his home and soured its sanctity.

"He had no idea where the treasure chamber is?"

Elas only nodded with a look of frustration to Rehema's question. This was the third guard the thieves had 'asked' of for the location of the mysterious treasure hoard and so far all three Northman either had no knowledge of the chamber or just chose a nap applied with the pommel of a dagger versus speaking. The Serval looked from face to face among the party, and now being the reluctant leader, she could easily see the doubt in each eye. Even her friends Lalya and Elas were beginning to show the misgivings for slipping into a lair where no one had any idea where they were supposed to go. Oh the pair tried to hide it but she knew both too well to miss the small signs and looks. Rehema sighed low, this was looking more and more like a lost cause to everyone in the party and yet the Anthros knew they could not give up. The life of Sefu depended on finding the treasure chamber. The Serval sighed again noting there was only one small piece of information which was worth anything from all the guard snatching the party had done this last hour. It was the location of more stairs leading down farther into the caves, what a young guard let spill before Elas put him to 'sleep'.

"Well, then we go down deeper into this place." Rehema

whispered turning to look out from the corner she hid at. There was no one in sight she noted as a harsh voice spoke up from behind.

"Is it wise to go down farther into this place?" Baldric asked.

"There is no choice, we cannot go back empty handed...either of us." Rehema answered without looking back to the human, almost refusing to acknowledge his existence. And why should she, the man had other plans she sensed separate from hers. He was here for another reason and Rehema did not care what that was as long as he stayed out of her way and let her retrieve this gem for Kazmir the Rat.

Baldric only snarled in silence at the obvious insult. Yes, little cat, enjoy your lead for the time I allow you to have it, for when my cue comes I will kill you the human thief thought while he glared at the back of Rehema's head.

He did not glower long at the Anthro because the Serval whispered just a blink before she broke from the cover of the shadows and moved down the passage. "Come, the way is open and clear."

The thieves all followed in one long line, the Anthros at the front and the Humans trailing, as the party silently travelled along the corridor. The line of beings darted in and out of the shadows moving low and slow but never too quick to miss the slightest sign or sound of an approaching guard. Then Rehema found the mark on the wall the guard had said to look for, just past a sconce on the wall, the mark for the hidden door. One glaring problem with using the Northmen for guards is most of the Odi lacked the smarts to find their own hidden doors, which is why someone marked this one. A secret is no longer a secret once it's been told and a door is no longer hidden when someone marks it because they cannot find it once said door has been closed. Rehema touched the surface of the wall and quickly ran her hand down the smooth stone looking for small button which would open the secret portal, and as she did Elas growled low. It was a signal, someone was coming, a guard most likely.

The Serval only hissed back letting her companion know she was moving as fast as she could. The moment, the time of it all, slowed to crawl as Rehema heard the sounds now of boots coming toward them from down the hall. Her fingers slipped along with the finesse of a Mage as she tuned her senses to detecting the slightest change in the feel of the stone. The boots grew louder. Lalya added a low growl of her own to the pressure of the moment which Rehema refused to answer due to the concentration she was using on her search. Then, just as the owner of the boots had to be just out of sight down the passage, the Serval found the button and pushed it releasing the lock on the door. As the portal opened she ducked inside without a look inside quickly followed by the others, the party disappearing a moment before an Odi appeared and walked by the hidden door without a glance in its direction.

The stair well was dark, barely lit by torches like the passages were, but it mattered little to the Serval. Rehema was as acquainted with moving in the dark as she was in the light, as were the other Anthros. The trio so quickly descended the stairs they created a gap between themselves and the Humans. Rehema scanned every step carefully before her feet touched each one, a necessary trait every thief must learn or face the disgrace of being caught...or worse. It was this trait which helped her spot the tripwire on the stairs, just like she did up on the first level of this place. Rehema jumped pulling her legs in to ensure she cleared the wire calling out in a low voice while she did, "wire!"

Both Lalya and Elas skipped over the wire with dexterous ease never once losing a step on their way down. Baldric and the brothers though, well the first jumped over the wire easily but then almost twisted an ankle when he landed awkwardly back on the steps while the second ones each stopped before gingerly easing their large feet over then moving on, obviously not wanting a limp as Baldric now had. The party soon reached the bottom of the stairs and stood ready by the exit, the Serval in the lead still. Rehema looked back opening her mouth to whisper a command to the gathered group. She was just about to tell them to stay quiet and let her lead them when bells and alarms went up echoing out in the passage past the portal. The faint sound of the same bells and alarms rang out above them along with the new sound of boots running to and fro...a great number of boots.

"Where did the alarm come from? Who set it off?" Fendrel yelped low.

"The dead body you left at the entrance, remember?" Elas spat just before the Fox next to him growled.

"Now we most certainly have too many guards!"

"It does not matter now, up above or down here. Come, we have to move before someone comes to use the stairs!" Rehema ordered opening the door and slipping out with a wisp of her tail.

The others followed just as fast keeping the Serval Cat in sight as she moved as fast as she dared keeping to the shadows once again. The party moved in single file down the passage quietly, but then Rehema spotted movement coming and hesitated just a moment. She looked left then right quickly trying to find a place to hide and found nothing in sight. There was nowhere to go and nowhere to duck so the Serval did the only thing she knew too, what her instincts told her to do. With a deep inhale Rehema hissed a silent order to her companions just as she flattened her body against the wall as much as possible. The dark of the shadows and hopefully her small frame dressed in black would hide her from the guards who were just a moment away. Both Elas and Lalya did the same, part order and part instinct just like Rehema guiding their movements. The humans cramped into the dark of the shadows too, not as well as the Anthros, but enough to hide and just in time as a pair of Trolls came shambling by, running to an unknown location. Rehema slowly exhaled trying as hard as she could to mimic being dead while pressing her body harder into the stone wall.

The thieves stayed as still as the grass on a day without wind as the two Trolls, one behind the other due to the fact the pair could not stand shoulder to shoulder and travel through the passage, passed the party without so much as a glance...until the one at the rear came to a sudden stop. It turned back and sniffed the air quickly while snarling low, menacingly at the odd scent it had just detected. The Troll at the front came to a stop as well and stepped back to its fellow monster with a grunt. "Why you stop?"

"You smell human?" The Troll at the rear asked looking to the green face still snarling just a little.

"Humans are all around us, Northman...Odi!" The first Troll spat now quite frustrated with the Troll he had been paired with.

"Not the same...these humans smell...clean."

The first Troll literally blinked in shock then shook its small head, "Odi wash...now we go!"

And before the second troll could respond the first turned and started to run again, heading toward its assigned unknown location. The rebuff did not stop the second troll which only kept talking as it ran to catch up. "When have Odi ever washed?"

"They wash, I see,"

"When," the second troll asked again?

"When we fix one for dinner," the first troll laughed, the sound slowly dying as it ran away from the thieves. The second troll only laughed as well quickly forgetting the new scent it had come across as it followed the first troll.

The thieves waited till the sound from the Trolls was no more before peeling away from the wall and finally taking a breath. Rehema only took a moment to regain her wits before slinking down the passage again slipping in and out the shadows created by the torch light. The party moved swiftly only coming to a stop once when a large wooden door with a small unidentifiable sigil abruptly broke the stone wall's facade. The thieves gathered round the portal waiting for Rehema who like before ran her fingers over the surface letting the delicate touch feel for any kind of trap or trip wire. A moment or two ticked away which only added to the anxious feeling the party was fighting when the Serval finally looked to them.

"There's no trap and no lock."

"Is it the treasure chamber?" Rolft asked quickly, too much hope in his voice.

"What kind of a treasure chamber has no lock and such a small door?" Lalya asked in a harsh whisper watching with some glee as the anticipation faded from the human's face.

"Have you ever seen a marking like that?" Elas asked staring hard at the sigil burnt into the wood of the entrance.

"Is it a magical glyph?" Baldric asked staring just as hard as the Canine.

"No," Rehema answered reaching out slowly and cautiously to run her hand over the brand, "I feel no magic in the marking. What it means, I do not know either? I have never seen such a sign as this before."

The thieves knelt huddled by the door, hesitating for just a moment more before Elas reached forward and opened the portal without a word. He slipped in ignoring the hard look Rehema gave him with a grin knowing well she did not like her leadership usurped but also relieved in the knowledge she would forgive him. They were exposed out in the passage while here inside the room they would have some sort of chance to develop a new plan for finding this hidden treasure chamber. And just as he knew would happen Rehema gave his arm a small pat as she scampered past letting Elas know he had made a good decision. The Canine let the humans by before closing the door to the room with a silent push, the only sound in the passage being the click of the lock. He turned and his mouth immediately opened in awe at the sight.

They had found a treasure chamber indeed, but not one which held one single gold coin or precious gem. No, there was nothing of the kind here. Elas was more than joyfully shocked into silence as he looked into a circular room with a stone floor. A single chair sat by small table with a large candle holder which contained numerous wax sticks with wicks already burning, as if someone had lit them then left. The mystery of who had done the task though was not even remotely in the mind of Elas. He saw the books on the table, a small stack, and then there was tomes on the floor sitting in a taller stack on a colorful tapestry and his heart raced. Yes, to the Canine at least, the thieves had found the true treasure chamber. As he crossed the room to the table quietly and quickly Rehema watched with a grin knowing her friend so well she knew they would have a time removing him from this place of knowledge.

"So, how do we find the treasure chamber?" Baldric hissed as the Serval watched Elas with a growing smile.

"I do not know. I only know we must or Kazmir will kill my brother and then you and I for failing to bring him the gem." She answered as Lalya walked over to the Canine.

The Fox grinned as her friend's tail wagged with happiness and then came to a complete stop as Elas looked deeper into the room noting the back wall was not a wall at all. What he thought was a stone wall was actually the end of a long shelf and next to it another and another next to that one. There were rows and rows of long shelves stretching deep into the back of the cavern and on each one were tomes and books and scrolls. There was so much here Elas thought breathlessly, so much I could never read it all in my lifetime.

"You know…I am still astonished that you know how to read my furry friend much less enjoy such a task." Lalya whispered still smiling.

"Of course I know how to read, and it is no 'task' oh my sister of pilferage." Elas responded now grinning as his tail wagged again.

"Really, and is that because you read to your love Drax as he lies with you in bed?" Lalya asked playfully with a raised eyebrow.

Elas chuckled stepping among the rows of shelves quickly disappearing. His fingers danced along the spines carefully just as Rehema's had done with the door to the room. "If you want to know yes, though I admit I enjoy the cuddling more when he falls asleep on my chest as I read to him." He called back from somewhere deep in the library.

"You must with his fine fur rubbing against you," Lalya chuckled too before looking over to see the way the Human brothers looked at her with a confused expression, "what?"

"The Canine, he lives with another male...Canine?" Fendrel asked in a whisper.

"Drax is a very handsome Puma Dae with tan fur, what of it?" Lalya asked quickly, harshly of the brothers. She did not need to hear or want to hear any talk of what she assumed was coming.

"His lover...he is a Feline?" Rolft asked back with shock.

The Fox looked from one brother to the next, from one bewildered expression to the other, before stepping up to confront them. "Does it bother you that my dear friend's lover is a male?"

Rolft sneered and shook his head suddenly as if slapped, "no!"

"It is not that," Fendrel remarked leaning in, "is it not odd to see a Canine and a Feline so...close?"

The truth made Lalya snort for a moment as it struck her. She smiled and chuckled before answering, "only because Elas is so ugly and Drax so handsome."

"I heard that!" The Canine's voice called out from somewhere among the row of shelves sending another snort through Lalya.

Rehema only smiled at her friends' antics with each other just as Baldric sighed, "if luck is with us maybe there is a map here amongst all those books which shows the way to the treasure chamber."

The Serval almost told the Human luck would have to be more than just on their side to find a map with the treasure chamber highlighted and noted. She would have made a good jest of the answer if not for the loud click the door made as someone was starting to open it. In a flash every thief broke into a dash and hid among the shelve deep inside the library as the entrance to the room swung open.

Six

This plan is insane...I should not be doing this, allied with this...but I cannot leave them to die...to sleep forever...

The words and thoughts ran rampant through Jura's mind as she travelled along through the passage, Voarothim just a step behind. They walked to the library as quickly as the pair dared trying not to draw any more attention to themselves than what was already occurring. Jura led the way keeping her eyes low barely acknowledging a single being as it walked by. There was the Troll Shaman who she nodded too as it passed, being one of the few followers who were allowed to speak to Thaxmosis she hoped it would tell him the Dragons were following his orders. She hoped the Shaman would tell the Terrible One the pair were fast making their way to the living quarters and not headed for the library. Jura was hoping with a small prayer Thaxmosis would never find out what she and Voarothim were about to do...then the alarms started to ring out and she came close to jumping out of her scales. Jura actually came to a complete stop in the passage and would not have moved another step if the young Red

Dragon had not put a hand on her shoulder reassuring her it was fine. The touch told her both were safe and it was safe to continue on.

If...when the Terrible One catches us...yet what if he does not...what if we find this book and then the antidote to the sleep poison Thaxmosis used on Palaxnym and Ith and he never discovers we have done so...what if we save them and they flee with Voarothim...would they leave me here with Thaxmosis...could I go with them...can I be free?

Again the words and thoughts ran through her mind, only now with the idea of freedom crossing the maelstrom of her thinking as Jura felt coldness down deep in her center while her heart skipped with sudden joy. It was terrifying and exhilarating at the same time, this sudden realization freedom was within her grasp. Oh to be away from the Terrible One, to be extricated from his influence...only where would she go? The world, the outside, it hated Dragons she had been told by others, by Thaxmosis. It maimed and killed our brothers and sisters little Jura. The world, the outside, it is dangerous and unforgiving while here inside this cave we are safe he would hiss in her ear. Here in my lair, our home, you are safe so do not think of leaving me, ever, my little Green Dragon.

"Are we close?" Voarothim whispered from behind.

The question from the young Red Dragon mercifully stopped the flood of words threatening to swamp Jura as she nodded and spoke low. "Yes, the library of the Thaxmosis is just ahead. He is not inside I hope."

"He will not be Jura, just take faith in that and nothing else for the moment."

Yes, take heart little Green Dragon that he will not be there...take heart this crazed plan of Voarothim and Palaxnym will work...only when it does will you stay or go? Can you hold to this courage and leave this place?

"Yes, he is not there," Jura whispered as they continued on and when the door came into view her gait quickened with anticipation, "here, this is the library."

Yet, just as her hand reached for the door to open it her nose picked up an unusual scent which stopped her instantly, Jura's fingers hovering just short of the portal. The Green Dragon breathed deep as Voarothim looked to her cautiously, "what is it?"

"Do you...does it smell like human?"

The Red Dragon looked at Jura confused for a moment, breathed deep though his slightly lizard looking nose, and then spoke low. "Yes, a very unclean human."

"As if they have not taken a bath in some days,"

Voarothim only nodded then looked around before speaking, "we need to continue, the book should just be inside, correct?"

"Yes, we will have to find it." Jura answered then opened the door entering the impressive collection of knowledge for one Thaxmosis. When the Dragons were inside the library, the scent of humans, and now Anthros, assailed them immediately drawing an instant reaction from Voarothim. The young Red Dragon growled again sniffing the air once then twice, "who is in here?"

There was no answer, nothing but the silence, and yet the Dragons knew better. Their sense of smell told them otherwise. Jura looked around scanning every shadow with her heightened sight and after a moment she found what her nose had detected shortly before entering the room. A face looked out from behind a row of shelves then, once sensing it had been seen, popped back behind the wooden holder. It was a human, yet then she saw another face look out, a Fox, and it was more than obvious who had set off the alarms.

"Come out," the young Green Dragon called out, "there is no exit from this place except the door behind us. Come out now!"

There was nothing but silence and non-compliance to her order and Jura was sure something foul as afoot. She could hear whispering and hissing coming from the room just beyond the small reading area, the thieves were planning something. Jura was about to order the intruders one more time to come out when Voarothim next her did just that with a little more...persuasion. "If you do not come out my companion will breathe a toxic gas into this room and the next. Then the decision not to come out will seem a foolish one as you choke to death with your eyes turning to liquid."

The personal athenaeum of Thaxmosis was quiet one last moment before a voice spoke up, a female one. "She can do that, breathe a toxic gas?"

"Yes, as sure as I can breathe fire."

"You really are Dragons then?" Another voice asked, a deeper male one this time.

"Yes, we are, now come out before I call the guards to pull you out." Jura demanded with exasperation. The question, having been asked and answered, was beginning to grate what little nerve she had left.

Then, slowly and with obvious caution, the six thieves came into the light with Rehema in the lead as she had been it seemed since this mess of a job had commenced. Her yellow fur with black spots glowed in the low torch and candle light as she spoke while looking up at the two beings who were at least a foot or two taller than she was. "You really are Dragons?"

"Yes we are, but why are you here?" Jura asked.

"We came to...acquire a gem from the treasure chamber that is located somewhere underground here." The Serval answered as truthfully as she wanted...as she dared.

Jura blinked at the statement, its veiled veracity, while Voarothim grinned slightly and whispered. "You came to steal a gem from the treasure chamber below here?"

"Yes, my brother is being held by someone who will free him if I bring them this gem." Rehema answered standing closer to the truth this time. "It is a large precious diamond with a blue sapphire in the center. It is said it-"

"-glows with the light of the moon," Jura whispered finishing the words for the Serval.

"That's the one," Baldric said with a nod.

The Green Dragon shook her head then and spoke, "do you know whose house you have broken into, whose lair you have invaded?"

The Anthros only shook their heads in answer before Voarothim parted the knowledge to them watching as the words struck each thief cold. "This is the house of Thaxmosis the Terrible One, the Great Black Dragon of Thathu."

"That does not sound good," Rolft said with a deep swallow.

"I didn't even know Thathu had a Dragon," Fendrel added with little flare.

"No, it is not good for you because the alarms have been struck and raised the guard! You would have never made the treasure chamber before the bells were rung, but now you most certainly will not! You will be captured and killed!" Jura hissed in anger.

"We did not set off the alarms. It was the other one who followed us inside the cave." Lalya countered quickly and then regretted even uttering a single syllable.

Voarothim's eyes went wide as he realized quickly what the Fox had said, "there are other intruders?"

"Just one...but he is..." Rehema tried to explain and failed to find the words. An Anthro which looked like every race, it was not possible, but there were the stories of the fabled ones from Pallator?

"Whatever he is, the being is as dead as you all are...as we will all be when we are caught!" Jura cried turning back to the young Red Dragon. Voarothim though was already contemplating how to use this intrusion to his advantage, but before the young Dragon could speak the door swung open as someone had the intention of entering. Ahead of even the quickest flash of instinct to run could tell Rehema and her party to hide the portal was open and the large body of an Ogre filled the entryway. Jura gave a yelp and stepped back into Voarothim who froze from the sight of the guard while his mind raced with panic. No, he could not fail. He and Jura had to find the Black Dragon's laboratory and retrieve the antidote to the poison. They had to revive Palaxnym and Ith...they had too...there was no other choice. The monster gave a low grunt which turned to an abrupt whine as it stared forward into nothing.

Then, as all those standing and staring at the Ogre were frozen with indecision, the body of the monster pitched forward or more like collapsed, as if it had been a very large tree felled in a forest. No one moved to catch the Ogre as it dropped like a stiff board face first into the room, its bulky body bouncing off the floor once before settling into a state of stillness. Jura's mouth fell open as did most everyone at the scene then with a flash a tall wide body slipped into the athenaeum closing the door swiftly and quietly. Every eye looked from the Ogre on the floor up to the new arrival, another uninvited guest, with an expression of awe. The new comer turned back from the closed door, spotted the full room, and smiled instantly at Rehema.

"Oh, it is you, how nice to see you again, unharmed and all."

The Serval blinked, twice in fact, at the sudden appearance of the being from the swamp, the one who had followed them into the lair and, well, the past is past she thought as she spoke in shock. "Who are you?"

"The better question is 'what' are you?" Voarothim whispered as he stepped away from Jura to approach the new comer. Just as his quick mind had realized what the Fox had said about another intruder the Red Dragon noted this was no ordinary Anthro or human who had appeared. No, this being was...special, and Voarothim knew just how special he was.

"My name is Jared Sinn and as for the second question, I am in search of that very answer at the moment." The new comer shared still smiling. He was not sure who to trust, the Anthros were honest looking enough, but the humans...the better path for the moment was to play this as though he was a proper fool.

The young Red Dragon stepped over the Ogre, who was alive the Wyrm realized because it was snoring heavily enough to send ripples through the carpet it laid on, approaching the new comer while ignoring the concerned look Jura was giving him. "Jared, do you not know what you are?"

"No," Jared remarked shaking his head playing the fool exceptionally well, "I do not, though I am aware I am a mix of all the races...somehow. Tell me, are you really a Dragon?"

The thieves stood perfectly still while staring as the Dragon and the stranger called Jared Sinn conversed. Rehema listened intently hanging on each word while behind her companions whispered freely between them.

"Reh told no tales, he is-" Lalya began before being cut off.

"-all of us, from head to toe an amalgamation," Elas finished.

The Red Dragon smiled brightly and nodded, the small visible scales on his neck poking out from the long mane of black hair which flowed off his head scrunching and squeezing like a splendid covering of chainmail. "Yes, I am a Red Dragon and Jura here is a Green Dragon, but you Jared...I think I know what you are."

"You do," Jared asked hurriedly with excitement producing the medallion he had been carefully carrying all these years and holding it up, "then you know what this means?"

The Wyrm reached up and touched the surface of the large ornament running his fingers along the carvings and then smiling, "no I am afraid. Those markings are words I am sure but none I have yet seen, though I think you might be better served with a certain tome for another reason."

"Why does he need a book?" Baldric whispered looking to Rehema.

"Yes, why does Jared need a book?" The Serval asked confused unable to follow where the Dragon was headed in the conversation.

Jura huffed with exasperation stepping up to Voarothim's side taking his elbow gently but firmly in her hand, "yes indeed, we do not have time for this!"

The young Red Dragon only smiled more though and chuckled as he spoke, "do you not see the coincidence Jura? I was to use the ruse of the Paracletus to gain the freedom of Palaxnym and Ith and on the very day I do we are visited by one of them."

As Jura gasped with surprise both Jared and Rehema spoke with the same shock, and right at the same moment.

"I am a what?"

"Jared is a who?"

Voarothim gave a small laugh and moved away from the stunned crowd and headed back into the rows of books. As he did Jura broke free from her bewilderment and smiled finally staring at Jared. "You are one of the magnificent Paracletus Jared, the fabled Protectors of the Races."

"I am a what, and slower this time please?" Jared asked playing the fool perfectly as the Serval stepped in closer adding her words to the mix now. It was just another confirmation of what he already knew, what the Weasel had told him, but the affirmation still made his heart race a little.

"All of the guardians are gone, dead, right? The stories the bards tell is none survived the fall of Pallator."

"I am the last of my kind?" The newly informed Paracletus, or so he let on, inquired with a snap of his voice.

"There were survivors Reh, some of the Paracletus escaped the attacks that night. Maybe Jared is one of those? " Elas answered with a smile and small wag of his tail.

"That would make Jared more than 80 years old, is that possible? " Lalya asked looking from Rehema to Elas and back.

"Wait, so I am NOT the last of my kind? " Jared asked

trying to stop the talk from going any father into how old he actually was. Now his heart was really beating, this was nothing new to hear, but these Anthros and Dragons seemed to know more than Jared had found on his own travelling the Lands.

"No, no you are not," Voarothim called out suddenly appearing from deep inside the library holding a book in each hand, "there are others like you Jared, only hidden now. The rulers and leaders of the Anthros, some at least of the five races, were rumored to have a sect of Paracletus secreted in a special location only those of royal blood know of."

With a fast hand Jura took the smaller of the books from Voarothim's grasp and then turned and offered it to a stunned Jared, "Here, this will tell you all you need to know. Cenloth was both a weasel and an accomplished historian who wrote down every story and word he came across about the Paracletus...including the night it all ended for the vaunted guardians."

"What do you mean 'the night it all ended'?" Jared retorted.

The Green Dragon shook her head though with a sad look hoping her concern and response would be enough to satiate the Paracletus. "There is no time to tell you what you need to hear Jared. Cenloth words in his tome will have to be your guide. Now please, we must leave for if a guard-"

"Too late," Fendrel called out with a harsh whisper from the entrance, "we have someone coming...someone very large and moving quickly."

"Where is the rear door to this room?" Lalya spat turning back to her companions.

"I told you, there is not one, which is why we should have left long before now!" Jura retorted with frustration and fear eyeing Voarothim with a hard glare.

The tension in the small library escalated hastily as it seemed each one wanted to voice their opinion and even a scheme to extricate themselves from the room. Rehema hissed loudly getting all under some kind of control and it was just in time as Jared looked up from the book he has holding with a careful grip. "You said you used a ruse about these Paracletus to free yourself from this place, have you told Thaxmosis already?"

"Yes, I have, but why?" Voarothim countered.

"Simple, I will be the distraction you all need to flee this room and hopefully this underground lair. I will find Thaxmosis and I will command his attention, all I ask for in return is for Jura to aid in helping the thieves." Jared answered slowly putting the book into the folds of his shirt and worn leathers.

"You will what?" Rehema and Jura both reacted together, their voices joining in the shock as one. Elas and Baldric both blinked and shook their heads in disbelief at the statement asking no one but themselves did they truly just hear that.

The only one who seemed to feel no confusion at Jared's words was Voarothim, the Dragon stepping close to the Paracletus to give a warning. "It is a dangerous thing to play a game with Thaxmosis. He is very old this Wyrm and his wits are as sharp as his claws. He is almost Ancient in age...he is no fool Jared."

"I understand friend, but I came here to speak with him so I am as ready as I can be. All I ask is for you to aid the thieves while I do."

Voarothim's face turned stoic as he contemplated what he as being asked, but it was only just for a moment before he turned to Jura. "The thieves were looking for the treasure chamber, tell them the best route to do so, please Jura?"

The Green Dragon bit her lip this time in contemplation as Fendrel at the door gave a hiss signaling the footsteps were close now. She shook her head once sending her long light brown hair tussling. The fight within her heart so evident Jared wished he could help more, but there was no time left to do so. He had made his plea. He had tried was all Jared told his own heart as he turned and headed for the door, stopping just as his hand touched the portal. He looked back long enough to speak. "Give me long enough to draw the Black Dragon away and then move with urgency."

"Thank you Jared," Rehema whispered and the last sight she had of the Paracletus was a flash of smile before he was out of the door. She turned to Jura then and noticed the struggle the Green Dragon was having had not subsided. "Please, do not make his gesture be for nothing, tell me where the treasure chamber is."

The plea was impassioned, just as Jared's had been, and yet Jura was still locked in a battle to speak a single word

The scents were strong. The intruders, Anthro and Human together, were close now which meant Thaxmosis was near in ending this heinous intrusion into his home. A very painful and excruciating end for all those involved, with the exception of him of course. He was actually looking forward to dealing out the punishment for the fools crossing into his domain without permission, and as expected the closer he drew to the thieves darkening his door his gait quickened. Yes, this would be-

It was then Thaxmosis realized with a dreadful dawning where he stood in his home and his fast walk slowed considerably. The scents, which were leading him down the passage, were heading directly toward his personal and very private library. The thieves could be, at this very moment, touching his precious tomes and books and scrolls. Grubby, filthy little hands and fingers could be touching his works of knowledge, his considerable collection of history and philosophy and theory could be in danger. The works of mages and chroniclers for which he spent centuries obtaining might be destroyed or worse yet...taken. The Black Dragon breathed deep, growled low in anger and turned to the Troll walking just a step behind. "If the intruders have reached my library I will have every head within my reach and my arms are long, do you understand me?"

The Troll gasped in stark terror and nodded so fast his cheeks actually flapped, but the sound barely covered the strong voice which suddenly spoke. All at once the sound stopped the Black Dragon's march in the hall while grabbing his attention at the same moment.

"Excuse me, but are you the one who all call Thaxmosis, The Terrible One?"

When the Troll spotted the tall being in the hall dressed in what looked like mismatched and ill-fitting leathers it growled and stepped forward screaming. "FOOL, YOU HAVE TRESSPASSED AGA-"

A large hand covered in small scales and ash colored slammed into the Troll's chest with a heavy and loud thud ceasing the monster's rebuke at once. Thaxmosis beamed at the being in the hall with a crooked cruel smile for he recognized this intruder instantly for what he truly was, even if this dullard of a Troll could not. Oh yes, he thought with a nefarious smile, is it not a wonder how good fortune favors the divine because look here, my very own Paracletus has appeared on my doorstep and right when I needed him too.

"Please excuse my follower. It seems the instruction on manners I gave him may have to be repeated." The Black Dragon answered trying as hard as he possibly could to be courteous and the effort was starting to strain his patience before it had even begun.

"It is fine. You are the one called Thaxmosis though?"

"Yes young one, I am he, but if I may, can I inquire of you your name?" Thaxmosis almost cooed. One of the Odi in the rear of the group blinked in shock, what he was seeing from the Master was...almost impossible.

The intruder looked to the Dragon with a side glance as he

measured in the others in the group with a sharp eye noting they were obviously taking stock of him as well. Thaxmosis patiently waited still smiling cruelly, though how much longer he would stay this way was anyone's guess. The Terrible One had little practice at being gracious thus the uneasy feeling of the followers. Jared could see, feel the Dragon already trying to connive and trick his way into his good grace, which was exactly what he anticipated. "My name is Jared Sinn, or so I have been called since birth."

"Well Jared Sinn," Thaxmosis moaned with dark pleasure as he seemed to glide across the floor to stand by this new treat without taking a single step, "I am very happy to meet you."

"Happy, even after I trespassed in your home...why is that?" Jared inquired cautiously, the sense that the walls of a trap were closing in around him filling his mind.

The Black Dragon only smiled on as he held out a hand guiding Jared down the hall away from the library, the exact way Jared wanted to go. "Oh all is forgiven young one, but please, come with me Jared and I will gladly answer all your questions."

"How do you know I have questions?"

"Well why else would you tempt danger and death to find me unless you have some pressing need...or inquiry?" Thaxmosis offered with a flick of his long tongue.

If it was not for the others waiting in the library to flee Jared would have run from this offer, evaded the mere mention of the barter and its originator. He could easily feel the malevolence flow off Thaxmosis, it threatened to squeeze the breath from his insides. Yet, there was no choice to make here. There was only one action to commit too. So Jared let Thaxmosis guide him away from the athenaeum and the others. He was sure there would be time to escape from the hands of Thaxmosis and in the end he did come here to speak to the Dragon, to decipher what the medallion meant, if he truly was one of the famed Paracletus. It was time then to hear the truth Jared decided. It was time to discover just who he was.

"Are they gone?" Baldric asked and to his relief Fendrel nodded before the thief continued. "Good, then I say we make haste and leave this death trap of a room."

"Not before we have the directions needed to find the treasure chamber." Rehema suddenly stated drawing every eye in the room to her and then to Jura. The thieves and Voarothim stared waiting for the Green Dragon to speak.

Only it was not that easy to go against Thaxmosis this quickly. Jura labored with each breath drawing each one like she was underwater, the air going no further than the beginning of her throat. How could they understand, this life as harsh as it is, well it is the only life she knew, the only way of living she had ever known. Jura looked from eye to eye as the thieves all waited to hear her speak and the fear which she had been fighting so hard to hold at bay began to squeeze the center of her soul with a frigid grip. How could they understand, if I do this I lose my home...I could lose my very existence. Then a had touched shoulder and Jura turned her head with a snap to see the large orange eyes of Voarothim filled with a deep compassion and more importantly a touch of comprehension.

"Tell them Jura. Everything will be fine if you do...trust me."

How could it be fine? Why should I trust you she thought? You do not understand what will happen when Thaxmosis finds the gem gone. And yet, like before when she had wanted to stop this idea of saving Palaxnym and Ith and could not deny the Red Dragon Voarothim, so it was again this time. She finally took a deep breath, finally took control of her fear and sent it away with a determined mental push as Jura looked back to the thieves. "The treasure chamber is to the east from here. Go out the door to the right and down the hall till it ends. There you will find a door marked with a rock in the center of different color then those anywhere else. Go through the portal, down a long set of steps, and the follow the winding hall from there as it will diverge more than once. The right path will be stone at first and then turn to roughhewed rock. This will be the marker to say you have found your way to the chamber, but be warned, the treasure is guarded by a powerful sentry."

Rehema took a mental note of every word and smiled once Jura was done. She knew it had taken an enormous amount of courage to tell the location of the chamber, more than the Serval could have imagined. She nodded and whispered as Fendrel opened the door to the library quietly, "thank you Jura. You have saved my brother, please take solace in that knowledge. He lives because of what you have done this night."

The young Green Dragon only nodded as for a moment she was overwhelmed with the abrupt feeling of happiness. Oh, she had not felt this way in so long, so very long. Jura only nodded back as the thieves slipped out of the room one by one, the Serval being last. There were no words Jura could think of, no response which would form in her mind. Only a silly smile as Rehema slipped away leaving her basking in the warmth of her joy. She finally turned to Voarothim and whispered, "Did you find the tome Palaxnym needed?"

"Yes, I have it." The Dragon answered holding up the spine to see.

Jura read the words there and her eyes went wide from realization, "The Chronology of the Wyrm, why does Palaxnym want such a work?"

"I do not know, he only said to ensure I retrieved it."

"That book is one of Thaxmosis most cherished, treasured tomes. When he finds it has been taken..."

Voarothim only smiled and nodded, "All will be fine Jura, have faith in our Gold Protector and his plan. Now which way to the laboratory, we need to get the potion to revive Palaxnym and Ith and we need to do it quickly."

Have faith, yes, I must have...believe in Palaxnym and his plan Jura told herself as she took Voarothim's hand in hers and both left the library. She led them down the hall toward the west, away from the treasure chamber and back toward the center of the lair. They passed more guards, Northmen and Trolls and Ogres, until Jura came to a quick stop. Only a handful of followers knew of the secret paths which wound through the lair, hidden walkways to move between the halls with expediency. Thankfully I am one of the few she thought as her long green fingers instantly touched a concealed spot on the wall. The button secreted there gave with a small click and a door suddenly swung inward revealing the passage inside. Voarothim's eyes opened wide at the sight, the door was so well covered the lines where it meshed with the wall were even imperceivable. He shook his head in amazement as he slipped inside the secret passage behind Jura and the door closed just a moment before a guard came by. The Northman never looked twice as he trotted by.

Seven

He was quickly lost in the twists and turns of the halls, which all looked the same to him at the moment. Row after row of the same stone block, each chiseled with the same carving and marking, turned the meandering walk into an endless flow of a common image and soon Jared was as confused as to which way was east as to which was north. And all the while Thaxmosis walked at his side talking in a low octave, each word and sentence laced with deception and deceit it seemed like, which only added to the confusion of where he was heading and walking.

"So Jared, you came all this way from the Endless Waste in the north to Thathu just to ask me about the Paracletus?" Thaxmosis inquired with the crooked smile still on his face. Hadn't Jared had just answered a question about where he had travelled from, or so he thought? The unchanging look of the hall, the slowness of the walk, and the tone of conversation, it all aided the Dragon in setting a trap and which added a tighter grip to the paranoia Jared was fighting to hold at bay as he answered the inquiry.

"Yes, from the mountains where I lived with my family or who I thought was my family." Looking around noting the Trolls and Ogres following were just a step or two away from protecting their master Jared chose his words carefully. It was just added paranoia and more pressure to the growing strain as he spoke. He had lied about his true origins to the Dragon and Jared felt no guilt from doing so. As Voarothim had stated, this was a dangerous game he was playing with a deadly adversary and he was watching where he placed every step carefully.

"Well, I am sure those who took care of you did so out of the goodness of their hearts. You were very young when the humans cared for you, were you not? Tell me, was it a man and a woman or just one or the other?"

Now this question was a little strange and Jared treaded around it lightly with even more care while trying to discern just what the Dragon wanted to know. "It was a man and a woman. I was the only child they knew, no sisters or brothers. Why do you ask?"

"Just curious young one, how did they come to find and care for you?"

"They did not find me," Jared looked back to where the

party was walking and taking a count of at least four more Odi who had quietly joined in with the group travelling the passage, trying to slip in unseen as they walked by. They are massing for an attack he deduced, and it will be soon Jared thought as he continued on with his ruse. "I was left in their care by a woman named Dreara one night. How I came about being in her care I was never told."

"Ah," Thaxmosis exclaimed with a nod and chuckle that sent shivers down Jared's spine, "she may have been a nurse maid for one of the Paracletus Women. The lady warriors were always more about war and fighting then the nurturing and rearing of their young."

"They were, why?"

"Really, has no one told you the history of the Grand Protectors of the Races?" The Dragon asked and when Jared gave a small cautious shake of his head Thaxmosis carried on. "The Paracletus were born, created some say, for one single purpose while alive and that was to fight and make war. Some considered them Knights because they protected the weaker Races in times of need while others called them warmongers because the Paracletus were said to have asked for gold in exchange for their protection."

Jared slowed in his pace, the words the Dragon had

spoken crashing into him like a rolling boulder. She had told him he was a Paracletus the weasel, one of the fabled guardians of the Races, so hearing it from the three Dragons did not shock Jared in the least. No, it was hearing the part referring to gold in exchange for protection which shook his very core.   All the stories his father had told him, the tales of bravery and courage, could it be all was done for gold? Could it be the guardians were never more than soldiers going to the highest bidder? "The Paracletus took gold in exchange for protecting the weaker Races?" Jared asked with a blink of his eyes in confusion.

"Yes they did young one, but do not judge your forbearers for such a practice too harshly. War and battle are expensive ventures to pursue and in the end does not one who risks life and limb deserve a reward for the undertaking?"

Jared counted each breath carefully and purposefully to keep himself under control, three in and hold then three out, as his head fought off the abrupt appearance of muddled feelings. Did he...come from paid mercenaries, was his sire and mother hired killers? "I did not know, these Paracletus, they fought for money...services rendered to the highest bidder? I have only heard tales of their forthrightness."

"When it was in their favor, yes young one, the Paracletus fought for money. Yet they were also noble and forthright, I admit begrudgingly. The Paracletus saved the Five Races during the Cataclysm for no reward at all, no gold or treasure. They heroically, and rather foolishly in my opinion, stood with the Anthros and evened the fight with the Mythical Ones and thus helped send the monsters back over the mountains to the Endless Waste. Is that not so my faithful followers?" Thaxmosis called out to the Trolls and Ogres and Odi who were following and walking beside them. Grunts and growls were the response and for a moment Jared was unsure if he was going to be attacked for doing nothing more than walking here in the group.

"They fought to save the Five Races...from these Mythical Ones? Who were they?"

Thaxmosis chuckled again sending another shiver down Jared's spine before answering. "It is what the Anthros call the ones who do not fit in with their 'Great Society'. The Trolls and Ogres are far too monstrous to live side-by-side with while the Giants-"

"There are Giants?" Jared asked so fast he gave no thought to the words before speaking. Again, only tales and stories had the young Paracletus heard about the strange and elusive 'Giants'. He had seen Ogres and Trolls before, when he travelled to forests and plains north of Thesedell where one could see the wilds of these Lands. He had seen Odi as well but Jared had never set eye on a Giant and for a moment his curiosity got the better of his control.

The Dragon looked to him with a raised eyebrow, as if the question triggered some mental trap in his mind. Jared instantly wished for the inquiry to have never happened, but it was too late for that he decided. He would have to be more careful with his actions from this point on he considered as Thaxmosis carried on.

"Yes young one, tall human-like beings which live in the hills and out on the Endless Waste. Some come from the hills while others from the frozen land farther north, but all have the same attitude toward any and all races."

"And what is that?"

"Giants want nothing to do with anyone else, be it human or Anthro or monster. They wish nothing more than to live in their little enclaves and be left alone." The Dragon answered and as soon as he had Jared was asking another question.

"But the Giants fought in the Cataclysm you said, right?"

"Yes they did, but after the Paracletus gave aid to the Races and drove the Mythical Ones back over the mountains the Giants have refused any kind of relation with any Race. It is for the better I say. The Giants have always been too smug and condescending a race to tolerate from my dealings with them."

The last from the Dragon barely made it through the thickening fog which clouded Jared's mind. He had come searching for his lineage and now that he had found a part of it he was uncertain he wanted to know much of anything else with it. These Paracletus, if you took what Thaxmosis had revealed with any weight, were nothing more than hired fighters and soldiers. How noble could one be if he or she fought for money? Yet, how could Jared trust a word the Dragon had told him? Everything he said went against what the weasel hold told him over the fire, went against the stories the human he called father told him back on the farm he grew up on. It was more than obvious Thaxmosis would lie to serve his purpose and need but the weasel…the man who raised him…were they lying too? Were they hiding a darker side to the fabled warriors, a history which might taint a reputation? So, he had come looking for his past and found what, a truth or a lie or both wrapped in a riddle? Those muddled feelings began to grow and harden as he carried on with the conversation.

"Why are Humans not part of the Five Races? "

The Dragon chuckled again, low and cruel, before answering. "It is because humans tend to be a part of both sides Jared and as such the Anthros feel little to no kinship with their close relatives, not enough to call 'brother' at least. Humans and

Anthros though have one foe alike in the Trolls and Ogres and Giants, it seems hatred of a common enemy may not make you a brother but it can make allies of anyone."

Jared nodded slowly accepting, somewhat, the words of the Dragon. There were human cities led by rulers throughout the lands, from North to South, and each one had Anthros living among them freely. It was the same for the great Anthro cities in the South or the cities in the West and East, small groups of humans living among the Anthros happily, though the Ursi and Burrowers kept to themselves. Few humans had ever seen the cities deep in the Mountains of the Cloudbreaks and there seemed to be a friendly acceptance between the Races and the Humans. Still, there was one question that burned in his head and the young Paracletus needed an answer.

"Where are the Paracletus now, why have I not seen any others?"

"It is due more than likely to what happened one fateful night eighty years ago Jared, a nasty confrontation between the Lord Supreme of the Paracletus and one of his underlings. Any survivors of the night have hidden themselves away to ensure their survival. I doubt, though, you have not heard of the fabled protectors before this moment Jared. I am sure you are very familiar with who you are and where you come from my young friend." Thaxmosis hissed menacingly while coming to a stop in the passage. He turned to Jared with a hard eye and a sneer.

Well, this game is over Jared thought as he looked over to see the Odi and Ogres beginning to walk past him, a secretive effort to encircle the prey. "Why do you think I have knowledge of these other Paracletus, if I may ask?"

"You said you were from the mountains in the North, which is a lie because if you were you would have a deeper knowledge of Giants young one. You would have also known of the Cataclysm if you lived in those harsh lands surrounded by the descendants of the very ones who were driven there, forced to live there now. Also, you have tanned skin, a sign of one who lives and works in the warm weather of the South. No young one, I think you know much more than you have let on, like maybe where the Paracletus hid their vast hoard of gold and treasure."

"No," Jared retorted while taking a step away from the Terrible One shaking his head, "I have no knowledge of gold or treasure. If I did I would dress better than a common...whatever."

"Yes I must say, the disheveled look led me astray for the slightest of moments, but then I realized it is just the way a spy would dress. You are smart young one, but I am Thaxmosis and I am very acute in my observations. I am smarter than any being you have ever encountered."

"And that is why I came here to your lair, to inquire of my past, because you are so knowledgeable Terrible One. The old mage in Thesedell who I spoke to told me to come and see you personally because you are the only one who could tell me...about me."

The words, meant to garner a small enough amount of time to aid in his escape, made the Great Black Dragon smile, though it was a more brutal grin then an impressed one. Thaxmosis stood in the passage staring as Jared took another step back to which the Odi and the Trolls followed by taking a step in the same direction. Oh yes, a new game was being played now as Jared stepped back once again followed by the others trailing him.

"And this mage you spoke to, tell me young one, was he drinking at the time he told you to undertake this crazed idea of coming here?" Thaxmosis chuckled which drew a small ripple of cruel laughter from the others.

"Not really, he just told me you might help with translating some markings." Jared smiled before stopping his retreat. He reached into his pocket and with deftness produced the medallion there with a swish of his fingers. The silver face with the words flashed dully in the torch light of the passage, the words inscribed there on the circular disc barely readable to the Odi and Trolls. Thaxmosis had no issue though with seeing the inscription and he had no issue with reading the arcane words. He had books in his library which were written in the same tongue so it was nothing to the Dragon to decipher what was carved in the disc, and what the medallion displayed shook his very center.

"No, it cannot be," the Great Black Dragon hissed with a whisper.

"Well now, that is a coincidence, the mage in Thesedell had the same reaction when he saw the words inscribed here on my medallion. He had the same look you have now old one so I can only assume whatever is chiseled here must be very...enlightening." Jared grinned, and then before anyone could react he was leaping backwards away from the foes which had the deadly intention of encircling him. In a flash of inhuman speed whatever trap the Odi and the Trolls and the Ogres had planned for Jared was lost as he sprang away, backwards some ten feet with what looked like nothing more than a subtle shift of his hips.

"He moves just like the Master, just as fast!" One of the Odi gasped with a hard whisper as the shock took hold.

"The offspring of the last Dominum Summum...it is impossible." Thaxmosis whispered taking a long step forward in bewilderment. In all his hundreds of years of age the Dragon had rarely been shocked to his very core, and today it had happened twice because at this moment he could barely breathe. Gareth and his line, it was gone, wiped from the lands by Hirall and his followers Cenloth had told. How could there be an heir? How could there be one alive who might raise the walls of Pallator again or command an army of the Paracletus once more? And yet there had to be an heir because he was looking at one, a true descendent of Gareth.

"How can he move like that?" Jared heard one of the Trolls whisper and in truth he did not know himself. He had always been this quick, this fast and strong.

He can move like me because he was gifted with our essence, a Dragon's spirit supposedly, or so Cenloth said in his book Thaxmosis thought as the dismay from the moment began to ween. Only the Lord Supreme can move that fast, that agile, because to rule gifted warriors one must be extraordinary to even them. Yet, what if this Jared Sinn was as crazed as his father was said to be and he did just that, took control of an unstoppable army? No matter the size, a gathering of Paracletus would most certainly draw the attention of the Five Races. The train of thought Thaxmosis was running with abruptly stopped when this herald of a new age of Paracletus spoke breaking his trance with a snap.

"Thank you Thaxmosis, for answering my questions and for your excellent hospitality, but I am afraid I have to leave now. No need to show me out, I can find my own way." Jared smiled now and using the same speed from before he spun and bolted down the hall leaving the Odi and Trolls standing in place, awe struck still. They barely had time to see the seven-foot-tall being disappear much less give chase, but the Terrible One was not done yet with Jared. He roared and launched after the fleeing Paracletus using his own unmatched speed to give chase.

The Trolls and Odi looked to each other with a surprised expression at the sudden shift in the Master's plans. What do we do now their gazes screamed before one of the Trolls turned and started after its master? As soon as the monster broke to run after Thaxmosis the others did the same and for a moment the passage was a jumble of bodies running into and bouncing off each other, weapons and armor clanging together loudly, until the dust cleared and the group was in full pursuit.

The Green Dragon Jura surely told the truth when she said there was a break in the passage leading to the treasure chamber, a fork she had said, yet what Rehema was looking at with wide eyes was so much more than a simple 'fork'. The thieves had followed Jura's words exactly finding the door with ease and then taking the stairs down to a simple passage with the same stone structure as the above halls. With quiet steps the party silently moved down the hall for what felt like an hour, the Serval impatiently waiting to see the stones morph to the rough walls of a cavern. Only the change never happened and then out of the semi-dark of low torch light the 'fork' appeared, all four new passages breaking off this main one, four new ways to go and not a track on the floor to signal which one to take. It was then, a tense Rehema thought, maybe the Dragon meant the stone would change in one of the passages and that was the sign the party was on the right path.

"Well, she did say a fork and there are four tines on a fork so..." Elas whispered looking at all four passages with his head cocked to the side.

"If I did not like you so much I would probably shoot you in the leg for even thinking of such an atrocious joke." Lalya replied with a chuckle.

The Dae chuckled with his friend as Rehema sighed with frustration at the two. It would certainly be most welcomed if she could have just one small bit of luck. She did not want much, just a sliver here or there, just enough to keep her from almost pulling all the hair from her tail, which was flicking side to side with angst at the moment. She stood trying to decide which hall to test when a voice made its owner's intent known.

"I say we send one of us down the left one, have the person go down a hundred or so steps and see what we find. If the walls change we can go on, if not, we come back and try the next one." Baldric offered chewing on his bottom lip.

The Serval turned to the human with a raised eyebrow, not out of dissatisfaction with the proposal but with surprise from hearing it or more to the point the one offering it. The idea was actually a very good one, and it left someone behind to ensure there was no 'backstabbing' or any such 'habit' an assassin looking to join a guild would commit. Rehema smiled thinking there were no words with more truth then those that stated by the Rat, 'there is no honor among thieves'.

"That is an excellent proposition Baldric, how do we choose who gets to go down the hall?"

The human smiled and nodded to one of the brothers. "Oh I heard Rolft volunteer, didn't you?"

"I did?" The brother yelped looking to his sibling with a worried grimace.

Fendrel shook his head and replied cold, "better you than me brother."

Well, maybe I did get lucky finally Rehema thought as she chuckled finally.

The laboratory of the Terrible One was impressive by any standard or rule of a master alchemist, but to one curious young Red Dragon it was pure astonishment. Voarothim stepped into the room after Jura opened the locked door and he came to a complete stop just past the entrance, struck numb by the wonderment. There were tables with odd looking instruments and strange glass jars and clay jugs, all of which piqued the insatiable curiosity of the Dragon, along the west wall. In the center of the room was a table with an assortment of long glass tubes connected to various other tubes which then ran over small candles, when lit would heat whatever was in the glass container, to finally end in even larger oblong shaped glass bowls. He smiled wide as Voarothim scanned the expanse of the room looking to the east wall where a set of long shelves ran the length of the wall, so many perfect nooks where more jars and jugs were kept in some special order by the Great Black Dragon. So lost in his own wonder at the sight it took a small shake from Jura to wake him.

"What is wrong?"

"Nothing," Voarothim whispered shaking his head, "it is just...I have never seen such a room like this. Does it not amaze you?"

"It did long ago, but once I witnessed what manner of destruction and pain this place creates for Thaxmosis…the enjoyment he derives from its evil…I have grown to hate its very existence." Jura answered sliding by the Red Dragon, nudging him firmly but gently to ensure Voarothim understood they had to complete what they had come to do.

The Red Dragon only nodded and followed fighting to keep his hands from feeling and touching every little object and glass tube. The smell might have been off-putting to anyone else but to Voarothim, it just added fuel to the fire of his curiosity. "Do you know what we need to reverse the effect of the sleep poison Jura?"

"No, I thought you knew what we required?" Jura snapped turning to face him with a look of fear and confusion.

"I do not know what is needed. This was not something Palaxnym planned for, being put to sleep forever. He assumed Thaxmosis would lock him and Ith away in a cell and wait for some important date before trying to kill them both." Voarothim answered with a shrug of his large shoulders.

Jura had no response save two long blinks. How in the name of all that she considered sacred had she let herself be pul-

"How may I help you Jura?"

The ghostly voice startled Jura and Voarothim making both give a yelp as a wispy cloud of smoke slowly drifted along the floor of the room. The Dragons watched, one eager while the other gathered her wits, as the smoke slowly rose and formed a human figure just a few steps from them. Jura had forgotten about the entity forever trapped in the laboratory by his own dark desires, the ghost of a mage who aids the Great Black Dragon concoct potions and draughts. A smile began to cross the Red Dragon's face as the Green Dragon answered the faceless specter.

"We are here...to retrieve the potion to wake the Dragons Palaxnym and Ith, Quatal." She spoke stammering a little at first before gaining more self-control with each word.

"You need to wake the sleeping pair, are you certain of that Jura?" The ghost Quatal asked in a sharp retort.

"Yes, Thaxmosis sent us to find the potion to wake them." Voarothim added moving to help the young Dragon. He sensed the reluctance in Jura and the suspicion she was receiving from the smoke form, a sharp edge to his approach and questions.

The specter looked at the Red Dragon with its featureless head speaking with a voice that seemed to come from nowhere in particular, "and you are?"

This was going from worse to a complete and absolute disaster Jura thought with a tinge of panic, and with the extra emotion pushing on her heart she responded before her companion could. "He is Voarothim. He has joined our master now, being that Palaxnym has been…removed."

"Really," Quatal spoke with a sneer in his voice which his featureless face would not show as the head turned from Voarothim to Jura, "but that does not explain why you are here asking for a potion to reverse the effect of the sleeping elixir?"

"It is for Thaxmosis sir, at his request." Voarothim took over again trying to convince the ghost of the lie.

It did not work as it replied coldly, "I think not, our master would not ask for a draught to reverse the effects of the sleeping elixir."

"And how do you know this, ghost?" The Red Dragon snapped with his own sneer, outwardly acting as if upset over being denied. It was all a play Jura recognized and she hoped greatly the ruse would come to a positive fruition for her and Voarothim.

The ghost Quatal only stood motionless as the fog that was his body swirled in its confined form. The grey-white of the smoke spinning this way and that inside the shape of a body usually captivated Jura, only this was not one of those times when such an occurrence would happen. A moment passed before the ghost spoke answering Voarothim with disdain. "I am my Master's assistant in all things Thaumagutary. I am his loyal advisor in all matters he asks of me so I know for a certainty he did not send you here for an antidote for the sleeping potion which affects the Gold and Blue Dragon."

"Come Jura, we will let the Terrible One deal with his 'advisor'. I am sure once Thaxmosis is told how we were denied he will rectify this with the ghost." Voarothim huffed guiding the Green Dragon to turn and walk away. The Red Dragon had gambled on this one move, a single chance at bluffing the entity into giving them the antidote to the sleeping potion. This had to work for if it did not…

She let him guide her back toward the door of the laboratory and with a small and reluctant first step. Quatal had to give, no one, not even a ghost wanted to face the anger of Thaxmosis. Jura took another slow reluctant step toward the door being led by Voarothim. The incorporate being that was once a mage would have to tell them where the potion was to reverse the sleep elixir because no one would willingly draw the wrath of the Great Black Dragon…surely not even a ghost. And yet that was exactly what Quatal was doing as he kept quiet watching with missing eyes the pair attempt to leave, for when it came to take a third step away Jura found her resolve slipping. She stumbled a bit, just a shuffle, yet it was enough for the ghost to see...and to chuckle evilly.

"What is the matter young one...has the courage of your conviction fled already?"

What do we do now she asked silently with her eyes as Jura looked to Voarothim? The Red Dragon stared back to her for a moment and in his eyes she could see the hesitation of what to do next. They were caught she thought, like flies to sticky paper, and the punishment would be severe for both. It was then, at that moment, that the years and years of being afraid of Thaxmosis finally came to an end for the young Green Dragon. All the years of being kept in the silent chains of fear and intimidation came to a striking and quick end as she turned and looked at the ghost growling low. She poured the anger which was building into her voice, into her will as she confronted the ghost.

"At least I am not his personal foot stool Quatal. You are a boor to think this station you hold is important to one such as the likes of Thaxmosis. He can have a hundred mages fill your role with a blink of his eyes and all better at magic and alchemy than you ever were or will be."

The words, like thrown daggers, struck home with unerring

accuracy. Jura had struck to the bone of the ghost, if the apparition had bones, and the swirling of the fog forming the incorporate body began to move faster. The undulating mist sped in a circular maelstrom as the anger in Quatal came forward in a flash along with his arm and finger pointing at the Green Dragon, his voice dripping with venom. "You will pay for those words Jura. I will watch my Master beat you, hurt you as he has done in the past and I will do so with a joyful heart."

"What is the matter oh witless ghost...have the words of my friend, the truth, been too much for your delicate nature to handle?" Voarothim chuckled suddenly pulling the featureless face to him.

"YOU KNOW NOTHING OF ME!" Quatal wailed loudly as the fog making up his body exploded, as if a storm was driving it every which way.

"He knows you are a useless mage Quatal, everyone allowed in this room has comes to realize this. I think, even if there were an antidote to the sleeping poison, Thaxmosis would never tell you how to prepare such an elixir. He regards you and your presence as unimportant as the Odi who guards the halls upstairs, an inconsequential follower to the Great Black Dragon of Thathu." Jura hissed with cruelty and oh, it felt so very good to let it go.

"HOW DARE YOU SP-"

"If you say there is no antidote then I have to believe there is one, there has to be." Voarothim sighed shaking his head.

The ghost made a sound which was like a growl only with a higher pitch and squealed at the Dragons. "Are you saying I am lying to you, that I am untruthful and dishonest?"

"In no way am I saying that," The Red Dragon sighed again shaking his head with a rueful grin, "but I do believe as Jura has suggested, that Thaxmosis would never tell you about an antidote to the sleeping poison because you are rather...well, inconsequential."

"I AM NOT!"

The anger which had boiled over from all the years of being treated as nothing turned now into an uncontrollable mirth for Jura. The Green Dragon began to giggle and chortle just slightly at the ghost's dismay, which in turn only infuriated the specter more. Quatal pointed his fingers at both Dragons and hissed like a snake with a nasal problem, "inconsequential, eh? I am boor, am I? Then how do I know there is no antidote to the sleep poison because it does not need one, eh?"

Jura stopped laughing almost before the last of the ghost's words were done, her eyes widening at the new information as she turned to Voarothim. "The sleep potion is only temporary!"

"The Terrible One lied to us…so that means… "the Red Dragon whispered with a growing smile.

The ghost looked back and forth between the pair waiting for his moment of revenge, for the come-uppance these two young upstarts had coming. Yet the only thing both seemed to care for was to look at each other. No matter, Quatal thought, the moment is mine no matter.   "I know this because I helped the Master create the poison! That is how I know!"

"We have to get back to the chamber holding the magical portal," Jura nodded while the beginnings of a smile formed at the corners of her mouth.

"Yes we do," Voarothim nodded with Jura and started to leave when the ghost behind them erupted finally. His sense of justice was unsatisfied, the wrong he felt committed against his character, however slight and possibly truthful, must be addressed and these two young Wyrms were to pay.

"I WILL SEE YOU BOTH PUNISHED FOR THIS EFFRONTERY! I WILL SEE YOU BEA-"

The last of the words of the ghost of Quatal, his soul forever trapped in a small box stored on the shelf along the wall, were lost to the mighty and frightful roar of the young Red

Dragon. Voarothim spun quickly attacking, his lower jaw unhinging like a snake's opening wide his maw, as fire flew forth from his mouth with a great rush and instantly devoured the fog that was the mage as he swept his head from one side to the other spewing flaming death. The conflagration enveloped the end of the room from the floor to the ceiling and any and all flammable objects burned or exploded instantly. In a blink the laboratory was fully ablaze as Jura gave a yelp then she was running with the Voarothim on her heels, fleeing the burning waste of a room. Both Dragons barely made the exit before some potion or elixir exploded behind them with more vigor than the others sending debris flying. They both kept running down the hall just a moment before the laboratory finally heaved one last time and this explosion shook the underground complex.

"Why did you do that, breath fire on everything?" Jura exclaimed with a gasp as the pair came to an abrupt stop. Smoke was pouring down the hall in black billows which flowed along the ceiling in waves.

"I could hold it in no longer, when the ghost threatened you I was angered and that seems to always lead to my breathing fire." Voarothim explained with a sheepish look.

"You were angered when Quatal threatened me...truly, no jest?"

The Red Dragon only nodded, embarrassed obviously from the sweet look Jura gave him, but then she was taking his hand in hers and leading them away from the ruins of the laboratory. "We have to hurry now and get to Palaxnym and Ith before the guards do."

Voarothim ran step for step with the Green Dragon following her every move as Jura ducked back through the same secret door in the passage from before. She was right of course. With the explosion of the Alchemy Lab every denizen of this dungeon would be sure to run to assigned posts now before readying to defend the lair and some might even try to stop them as they ran to help Palaxnym and Ith.

Eight

The glen was not real. This grass she was laying on...it was not real even though it felt just like what one would find in a meadow, what she had walked across barefoot not so many...was it just a day or a month ago? Ith fought the need to sleep, to drift off into a deep slumber, but it was so hard to struggle with the sweet desire to hibernate. She breathed and shuddered as the poison in her system demanded she give in and fall sleep before whispering. "Palaxnym...we have...Voarothim is...alone."

The Gold Dragon, still leaning against the face of the boulder, only sat breathing steadily as of the words from his companion either were not heard or were not enough to warrant him to move or waken. A moment or two passed before Ith spoke again, louder with all the strength she could gather.

"Palaxnym...Voarothim...Alone!"

Finally, the Dragon stirred as his eyes fluttered open, "He will be...fine...poison is...awake soon."

And as Palaxnym's eyes closed again and he slept a small sweet breeze blew through the glen, though from where might have been a good question for one to ask. Ith though was no longer able to inquire about this riddle of the magical space though as she finally gave in and rested in the crook of her companion's arm.

Almost out of breath, the Trolls and Odi finally reached the spot where their Master had stopped in the passage. The Ogres trailing behind stumbled up huffing like mad as one of the Northman gasped and spoke. "We are...here...Master."

"I can see that!" Thaxmosis hissed standing outside a door in the wall of the passage. The door did not look like any other on this level, being metal and not stone or wood. Large Iron bands kept it in place as the Black Dragon pointed to it angrily. "What is this room?"

The Odi looked surprised and then more than a little scared as he turned to the Troll next to him refusing to answer the question. Thaxmosis turned from the Odi to the large green Troll who was now leading it seemed with the same angry look. The monster coughed suddenly finding it just a little hard to speak, "It is an armory Master, your Armory full of swords and axes and hammers!"

The answer caused the Dragon to step back in shock, first staring at the door for a moment before turning back to his followers with a raised eyebrow. "I have an armory on this floor?"

"Yes Master," the Troll nodded cringing just a bit.

"When did I order this?" Thaxmosis demanded, back to being angry again.

The Troll turned at the look from his master to the Odi handing off the Black Dragon's question to him with a shake of its head. The Northman turned away from the Troll swallowing hard before speaking and answering, "a year ago I think Master."

Yet again the answer sent Thaxmosis rearing backward just a little as he hissed, "A year ago...really?"

This time the Odi cringed, his whole body locking in place as his eyelids slammed shut and he mumbled over and over 'please don't melt me, please don't melt me'. The Black Dragon though made no move to melt his follower, only turned to the door and glared at it. "The Paracletus I was chasing, he ducked into this room and barred the door from the inside. How do we get in there?"

The Northman's eyes opened with a blink as he looked back to the Troll and shrugged his shoulders, the gesture saying it is your turn now. The Troll blinked as well and looked back to Thaxmosis, who had cocked his head to one side staring coldly at the pair. It was starting to undermine his waning patience how these two kept passing the torch, or the question, back and forth between them. The Troll though finally spoke after gathering his courage.

"There is no other way in Master. The room is built to secure weapons so the only door made to come and go is that one."

The Black Dragon's head slowly twisted going back to normal as Thaxmosis glared at the Troll and Odi, "there is no other way into this room you are telling me?"

The Troll looked back to the Odi who then turned to the others in the group and all looked back shaking their heads. Well, this was the final straw, the final piece of what felt like a mountain of misfortune and ineptness which sent the Black Dragon into a seething rage. He growled low ready to unleash his pent up fury with a single release of his acid breath, only a voice yelled back from inside the room and unimaginably the Dragon's fury grew even more.

"You know Terrible One, there are some very nice

weapons in here. I see a nice sword or two, a whole rack axes and maces, and in the corner is a spear that has caught my eye. The shaft of the spear, what kind of wood it made from?"

Oh, now you have finally struck my last nerve Thaxmosis thought with blood thirsty anger as he turned to the stone door. "Then take what you want Dominum Summum and come out here. Prove to us all what I already know, that the sins and madness of the father always fall to the son."

The hall was suddenly very quiet, the only sound the breathing of the ones occupying it, and all staring at the portal. Thaxmosis was sure his little statement had piqued something inside the mind of the one barred inside. You came looking for your past Dominum Summum, well then, let me lay bare all of the abhorrent deeds that is the house of Gareth the Dragon thought smiling cruelly once again as a Jared spoke finally through the door.

"What do you know of my father?"

"I know quite a lot about him Jared, but why should I share my valuable knowledge with you young one, especially through this metal door?"

"Because I will tell you what you wish to know, what you need to know Terrible One. I offer a fair exchange, you tell me of my father and I will tell you about a hoard of gold and treasure the likes you have only seen in dreams." Jared proffered quickly and the barter was more than tempting, though not at first.

"You know nothing of a treasure and gold Jared Sinn. You would lie to save yourself."

"That is true Terrible One, yet I know things of importance just as you. I have not shared the truth of my life to you, what I have been told by the ones who raised me or what they left me other than this medallion. What harm would a trade bring? It is much less than the risk of you losing all the gold your heart desires, right?"

Thaxmosis stood quiet staring at the stone door. He could easily rip it from the wall, his strength was unmatched and with his anger fueling his might there was no portal he could not cross. Yet, could he chance a fight with the Paracletus on the inside? He had lied about being raised in the north but maybe he would part with some small piece of knowledge which would lead him to the gold? An exchange might be the best approach because what if something happened and Jared met an untimely end, well, before the boy had chance to speak of this gold at least. He was always going to be killed the Dragon thought before making a decision.

"Agreed then, but know this Jared, if you think you can outwit me then give up on the folly of trying. I am smarter than you and if you force me I will have my followers encase you in that room to starve and die alone in the dark, understand?"

There was another moment of silence, contemplation the Dragon assumed, and then Jared was answering. "Agreed and understood, now what do you know of my father."

The cruel smile only grew and the spitefulness so outwardly showed on the Dragon's face the Odi and Trolls and Ogres all shivered at the sight. Thaxmosis leaned in and whispered, almost like a lover into the ear of one's desire. "Your father, Gareth, he was crazed young Jared. He inexplicably turned on the very ones he was born to protect, the Races of Anthros. He threatened to lead his Paracletus army into every grand city of each race and destroy it, killing everything he could and burning the rest. When he was stopped by his Vicegerent Hirall is when the depth of his insanity was truly discovered. Gareth killed his own people, he murdered his loved ones and brought about the destruction of all that was meant to protect the Races. Your father young Jared, he was as much a monster as the Trolls and Ogres and the Odi that stand out here with me."

Inside the dark of the armory, the one torch barely keeping the shadows back, the trembling hands of Jared barely held onto the medallion. He could barely hold it, the words of Thaxmosis turning this one link to his past from a treasured object to a cold piece of metal filled with horror. The Paracletus were no longer the honored knights he had envisioned and now this? My father...he was a monster?

"Is something wrong young Jared, are you shaken now? Have I told you something you were not ready to hear? Do not tell me, you had this cherished dream of your father and your past but now it is broken, like shattered glass on the floor. Oh, truth be told, I am not very sorry young Jared."

"My Father Was No Monster!" Jared screamed back as his fist closed around the medallion and squeezed so hard the metal disc threatened to bend and break. No, his mind screamed and his soul howled, this is a lie, a deception meant to lure me from this sanctuary and out into the passage. All of his words, every last one was a lie Jared growled silently, it had to be. And yet the anger he felt, the same rage the Black Dragon had used felt just moments before, pushed on his heart to be let go. Suddenly he wanted nothing more than to snatch up one of these swords or axes or the spear and wade into a bloody confrontation with any and all in the passage.

"Oh but he was young Jared, he was. Here, let me tell you how your mother died to show you. She was killed by your father in a barbarous and savage attack. He beat her and then stabbed her to death before turning his knife and sword on all the others in Pallator. He killed the innocent and the unarmed alike, sending all to their deaths with screams of pain and betrayal. If not for his Vicegerent Hirall stopping him your father would have attacked the Anthros and slaughtered so many more." Thaxmosis hissed as the venom in his words stronger it seemed now.

He is enjoying this, wallowing in the misery and the pain he creates with his forked serpent tongue. Well, Jared growled as he squeezed the medallion even harder, I will give you crazed. I will show you the sins of my father he thought with a bloody vision of hacking his way through the Dragon's followers, but then a strong ghostly hand touched his shoulder and the melodic words of an angel whispered to his heart and soul. It is a lie my little one the words soothed, you know this from our last act to save you. Instantly the anger, the overwhelming blood thirst, disappeared as Jared let the peace of both reach into his center and take away the violence and outrage. He breathed deep this serenity and smiled slowly looking down to the medallion in his opened hand now, whispering. "I know you were no monster father...you could never be."

"There young Jared, I have told you what you came searching for, now come out of the room and tell me where this hoard of gold is."

Yes, you have told me of my father Terrible One, your

version at least. You have more than lived up to your end of this nefarious bargain, Jared thought, so let me live up to mine. He leaned over and took two of the short swords off the rack strapping both to his back, the hilts over the right shoulder. Then he reached over and took one of the maces off the rack and placed it in his belt in the front. Waging war, I was born to do it you say Thaxmosis, well then it is time to see if that is the truth.

"What are you doing young Jared? Are you backing out now of our bargain?" Thaxmosis inquired through the metal door.

"No Terrible One, I am not backing away from our bargain. I take it you still wish to know where the hoard of gold is." Jared asked stepping close to the door.

"Yes, you know I do!" Thaxmosis spat beginning to feel his rage grow and blossom once again. "Now tell me where I can find it!"

"You will not have to go far for it Terrible One, the great golden hoard of the Paracletus is very near." Jared remarked a moment before two gold pieces came sliding out from under the door.

What was this, Thaxmosis questioned silently as he stepped back from the two coins. The followers of the Great Black Dragon looked down at the coins in disbelief, most thinking the fabled Guardians of the Races must have been very poor when they perished if all they possessed were two coins.

The young Paracletus could almost imagine the look of confusion on the Dragon's face as it was now his turn to twist the knife and Jared had every intention to dig and turn the blade. What kind of a jest is this, Thaxmosis mind asked as Jared continued on?   "It is all I have with me right now Terrible One but I am sure I can get more if given time, oh, and the chance to leave this room."

A shudder and a gasp went through the Dragon as he stepped farther away from the door in bewilderment and shock before the anger in his heart boiled once again. The Trolls and Odi and Ogres in the passage gasped as well for none had ever seen their Master this angered before, as if at a loss at first before snapping to the visage of his old name, the Terrible One. Thaxmosis snarled and shook with pure fury as the young one in the Armory kept talking as well, each word like an arrow shot from a bow.

"Are you still there Thaxmosis or have you given up yet?"

"I warned you, mock me at your peril Jared, now I will kill you without hesitation." The Dragon growled ignoring the question and its intended purpose which was to dig under his scales even more.

"Then come Terrible One, be the first through the door so I can test my mettle and spill your blood." Jared answered with his own low growl through the door.

The snarl, which like his anger was growing with each quick breath the Dragon took, deepened and came from somewhere deep in his chest. Thaxmosis let the response form the Paracletus drive his rage to unknown levels as his body began to shake with the exploding fury in his center. His teeth gleamed from lips which were pulled back with furor, the acid building in his chest was ready to be released in his ferocious breath attack, but before the Terrible One could do anything the very floor and lair walls shook with the effects of an explosion from somewhere farther inside the Dragon's home. Abruptly the need to destroy young Jared was lost in this new predicament. Thaxmosis turned away from the door to the Armory with a jerk of his tall body and looked down toward where the rumble had come from.

"What was that?" One of the Odi asked with eyes wide.

"I think it was the Master's-" one of the Trolls began to whisper with shock.

"My Laboratory...someone has done something to my LABORATORY!" Thaxmosis screamed in dismay and anger.

There were other intruders, more than just this fool of a

young Paracletus and the slow-minded Palaxnym and his group Thaxmosis screamed again silently to himself. There were other intruders, different invaders who have now committed a truly foul deed. I should have known a young one like Jared was no thief, he had no true skill to enter my lair unseen, and Palaxnym and Ith were both taken care of so who-

"Jura and Voarothim," the Dragon growled low with returning rage. The names rolled from his mouth with that anger as he began to understand who had truly invaded his domain. His mind dredged up image after image with ease, showed each picture to his mind's eye of the nefarious acts both young Dragons had done to him, and with each breath the fury for Jared switched to Jura and Voarothim. "Those two will pay for what they have done this day..."

"Jura Master, she has something to do with this?" The Troll who led the small group asked with a careful inquiry after hearing the name of the pretty Green Dragon. He, and everyone else, could see the Master's rage was beginning to become uncontrollable and as such you better be careful where you stand.

"She and that traitor to his kind Voarothim," Thaxmosis hissed and turned to the Troll causing the monster to jump a little. "Get Jared out of MY armory, alive or dead I do not care anymore. I will deal with our treacherous Jura myself."

Then he was gone in a flash, the strength of his legs and the power of his body propelling the Dragon forward and out of sight in a blink. The passage was quiet again, well as quiet as it could be with the alarms still ringing out, as the Troll looked to his fellow followers and spoke. "We need to find a way into the armory."

"I'm not going in there," an Ogre said with a shake of his head eyeing the others with a fearful eye, "and anyway how do we break down a metal door?"

"Are you saying you're scared Ogre, of a boy?" The Northman who spoke before called out with a harsh laugh taunting the large beast. He moved to the door examining the portal with a careful.

The monster growled and shook his head ready to cut the Odi back with a quick retort when the Troll who led them cut him off. "Shut up all of you! We have to find a way into that room or our Master will melt all of us!"

"I think if we break the iron bands the door should just fall off," The Northman stated chewing on his bottom lip as if in deep thought.

"And what do we do with the Paracletus inside, the one who has armed himself now with our weapons?" The Ogre retorted with sarcasm, or as much disdain as an Ogre could muster.

"That boy is no Paracletus Spit," The Troll hissed shaking his head. He swore under his breath about the ones he led. Some days he'd rather lead a bunch of Dae's on a flower picking-

Before anyone in the hall gathered in a loose semi-circle could react, the very door they were debating on how to remove suddenly snapped free of its bands and toppled over with a loud crunch into the passage. It fell right on top of the Odi who had been studying it diligently crushing him beneath its weight and leaving just his forearm and hand pointing down the hall to where Thaxmosis had bolted. And on top of the portal, standing tall where both his feet had landed when he kicked the door with both boots setting it free from its moorings, was Jared Sinn glaring like a mad human at others in the hall. In one had was a sword while in the other was a mace, strapped across his back were two more swords, and a malicious gleam in his eyes as he snarled. "Where is the Terrible One, we have a discussion to finish?"

Thaxmosis had never placed much faith in his followers to do much when it came to defending him. He was never fooled into thinking any of the dark souls who found their way to him and his lair buried in the swamp were any type of a hero. No, he had no delusions when it came to his 'devoted minions' one might call them. And it was quickly proven when all of the Odi and the Trolls and Ogre who had trailed along with Thaxmosis and Jared just moments before broke and ran screaming down the hall away from the Paracletus. It would have been no surprise to the Terrible One to see his guards fleeing while yelling loudly they did not want to die a gruesome death. The only one shocked by the display was Jared, who sighed and shook his head.

"All right then, I'll find him on my own if I have to." He stated with a sneer before running after the group. The door, resting on the Odi, only shifted slightly as the Paracletus took off in a dead run.

Nine

———— • ————

"Am I the only one finding it hard to breathe right now?"

Lalya's words only echoed what Rehema and the others were feeling, struck literally and physically dumb from the sight of the Dragon's treasure chamber. There had been dreams, for both the Andros and the Humans, of gold piled high to ceilings and gems the size of one's fist scattered throughout a large room. No dream could equal what they were seeing now though. No vision could touch this reality, not even the wildest of the wild. The Serval stepped into what was easily the largest chamber she had ever been in, larger than any built with the hands of an Anthro or human. The ceiling was easily twenty feet overhead and the rear of the cavern would take at least a thousand strides or more to reach and along that walk were piles and piles of gold pieces and jewelry and anything else which gleamed or sparkled. Everywhere she looked Rehema saw a pile of treasure or an item of value, everywhere she looked.

"How are we supposed to find the Eye of the Moon

amongst all...of this?" Fendrel whispered turning in a loose circle bumping into his brother as he spun uncontrollably, who was standing still in stunned silence as well. The question was not answered because no one had thought of such a problem existing, a problem by the way which only seemed to grow worse as Elas spoke.

"There is another chamber beyond this one."

A collective gasp went up as all eyes turned to follow the direction which the Canine pointed. There, through a large opening, a second large circular chamber could be seen and just within the opening more piles could be seen, more gold and treasure. It was too much Rehema thought with a panic, so much wealth in one place...almost too much. The fear of finding too much gold had never crossed the Serval's thoughts, ever, but now suddenly the feeling pushed in on her lungs making it hard to breathe. Then Baldric spoke and that feeling of fear gripped her even harder, squeezed like a coiled snake.

"There's one over here as well."

"Three chambers...who has three treasure chambers?" Rolft asked with a whistle as he looked at the third chamber, the entrance the same as the second.

It took only a moment for Rehema to answer, her

response filled with dread now, "a very, very, old Dragon."

"What Dragon...like those two back with all the books?" Fendrel asked looking as if the Serval's response was filled with crazy.

"No," Rehema replied choosing not to make eye contact with the human as she scanned the chamber and pile after pile of gold, "nothing like those two. If we have the unfortunate fate of crossing the one who holds this hoard dear, then you will know true terror."

The thieves stood motionless just a few steps inside the treasure chamber trying to discern and formulate a plan to do exactly what Fendrel had asked about.   How does one find a needle in a stack of needles, especially when all the needles were precious gold and the only thought in your mind was how can I take ALL of this with me? Rehema sighed as her tail twitched with anxiousness. This kind of a search would take a full change of the seasons she told herself silently as something ran across the toe of her boot. The Serval looked down to see a large hairy spider scamper between her legs heading off behind a large pile of gold pieces with a few boxes of jewelry sitting on top of the mound. It was nothing to note, not really since she was not afraid of a little spider quickly searching for a place to hide from the ones who were now invading it's home. Rehema smiled thinking she had never been afraid of creatures like spiders and centipedes and such, and then she saw another large spider slipping with dexterous ease by Baldric heading for the same pile of treasure. Now this was something to note, two spiders heading for the same pile, but the pair was not alone she quickly realized as three beetles and a scorpion were all making a line toward the same pile of gold. The scene raised the alarms in the Serval's mind as she whispered looking around the cavern.

"We are alone here, we checked for others did we not?"

The answer which came from Baldric was as far from reassuring as it would have been for her to suddenly trust the human. "I could look no further than these piles of gold for anyone or anything to be truthful."

Now the alarms in her mind were wails of fear as Rehema turned looking all about the room, searching for the one being she knew had to be here. She was just a blink away from asking Lalya to sniff the air for a scent when Elas spoke up with a growl, his large hand reaching down and grasping the hilt of his short sword. "Do you hear that? Someone is chanting!"

And like a strike of thunder the crash of realization in her mind caused Rehema to gasp. Fools, she hissed outwardly as her thoughts screamed, we are bunch of young fools! We walked right into a trap she knew as the Serval yelled out loudly. "Spell

Caster! There is a Mage in here with us!"

The warning brought an instant reaction from the other thieves. Lalya drew her hand crossbow with a snap as the human brothers both filled both their hands with daggers and Elas unsheathed his short sword with a quick pull. Rehema looked right to the pile of gold knowing already the one who was chanting was behind it. How long had the Mage been back there chanting she questioned? The longer the chant the more powerful the spell she knew as she took two steps forward while pulling her long dagger from its sheath. How long have you been there Mage waiting to strike she wanted to scream, only the one she feared appeared abruptly cresting the top of the gold with a small step sending coins sliding down its slope. This was no spell weaving Mage this one though, no, it was worse and as Rehema felt her heart slow and her blood cool while Lalya gasped from behind with fear.

"It is a Troll Shaman,"

Yes, now the Serval knew why the spiders and the beetles and the scorpion fled toward the gold pile. The little ones were not escaping to safety...the small vermin were being called to the Shaman's side. The insight was barely formed in her mind before Baldric was screaming out an order, a silly one at that. "Kill the Troll! Kill it before it finishes!"

The Anthros only stood eyeing the Troll as it kept chanting in the strange words of its kind while the humans all snapped into action. Fendrel and Rolft both reared back and threw one of the daggers in their hands, the blades speeding in a tumbling line right for the chest of the monster. Rehema knew before the weapons struck the Troll the attack was useless, fruitless as her sharp eyes picked up on the monster's skin. It's usual green tone was a deeper shade of grey now and the hair running over its head and back looked stiff and solid. The Serval knew instantly what this meant and she watched helpless as the daggers hit the monster square before bouncing off. Both the brothers yelped in shock stepping back and once more Rehema watched helpless as the Troll's chanting came to a stop and its beady eyes stared unflinching at the thieves.

"What's it doing now?" Baldric whispered low, his voice filed with worry.

"I think it just finished what it was doing and I have a feeling it will not make us happy in the least." Lalya answered even though the question was not for her. Her words were barely done when the first clicking sound came and then another and another. It just might match the sound a small creature crawling across the ground might make when its long legs touched a hard surface, if one could hear such a thing, or maybe a step on a pile of gold, only louder.

"We need to flee Baldric, now!" Rehema ordered just as the first of the spiders that had fled behind the pile appeared again, only now it was much larger in size, as big as one of us the Serval thought with growing fear. Then slowly the second spider appeared on the side of the Troll and then the beetles and finally the scorpion. All the small vermin were now larger, grown in the blink of an eye by the arcane magic of the Shaman to a giant size. As the thieves stood staring at the group of large monsters surrounding the Troll Baldric whispered standing next to Rehema's side.

"I agree, fleeing is our best option."

The thieves took a small step back, away from the pile, and the vermin and Troll only watched with an intense stare. The thieves took a second step back and this time the Shaman stepped forward raising his arm, pointing the limb right at Rehema. Damn, she thought, we walked right into this!

"KILL THE INTRUDERS!" The Troll suddenly screamed and the vermin howled in a high pitched scream of their own while charging at the thieves.

Jura led Voarothim as both the young Dragons ran down the secret passage appearing out into the chaos of a hall, Trolls and Ogres and Odi running to and fro. Not a one of the Black Dragon's minions seemed interested in the pair and Voarothim was just a little elated at that fact. He was sure both he and Jura were in more trouble than he could anticipate after destroying Thaxmosis's laboratory, and yet with all the pandemonium at the moment not a soul was looking for them. Jura headed south down the passage and he fell into step keeping up with her easily while dodging everything else, monster and human alike. The funny part of this, if there was some hilarity to be found, was he starting to recognize pieces of the passage they were in, given just a little longer and he might actually have learned his way around.

"We are still heading to the cavern for Palaxnym and Ith, are we not?" Voarothim called out while missing the jutting shoulder of an Ogre as it passed by.

"Yes, the entrance is ahead a little farther," was all Jura offered as she continued to move along the crowded hall pushing Northmen aside and ducking Ogres. If everything went precise, if they were fast enough, then she and Voarothim could get the magical lantern which held the Gold Dragon and his mother Ith. If luck shined on them just a little longer than they might live and see this to the end.

So they ran on pushing through the followers of the Terrible One until the entrance to the cavern where they would find the magical lantern appeared. It was nothing more than alcove the entrance was, a small break in the passage and most if not all of Thaxmosis's guards passed it by without a second glance, yet Jura ran right toward it slipping inside without slowing. Voarothim followed never slowing a step either as he watched Jura reach the back of the alcove and then run right through the end of the small break. It was an illusion the wall, another one of the Great Black Dragon's tricks to ensure the secrecy of his lair. Only a few knew of the cavern here Voarothim thought as he ran through the wall feeling only the slightest tickle as the magic of the phantasm touched him. Then the Dragons were running up the small incline to the cavern and before either could catch their breaths the lantern was there, still sitting on the flat top of the small cone shaped rock formation. Without hesitation the Red Dragon reached for it intending to open the small door and thus open the gateway to the magical space where Palaxnym and Ith were being held. Only, for some strange reason, the door refused to budge or open even in the slightest. He tried once then twice before realizing the small portal was not going to open for his fingers.

The fumbling did not go unnoticed as Jura spoke, "what is wrong, open the door?"

"I cannot…it refuses to move." Voarothim replied while trying a third time to open the charmed lantern.

"Just open it, here let me try." Jura stated impatiently while stepping in pushing Voarothim away. She began to try and open the door and only found the same results, the small portal would not budge at all. Once then twice she tried to no avail, nothing it seemed was going to open the door she thought as her friend spoke.

"What if we smash it open?"

Jura shook her head, "no, we cannot do that. If we break the lantern it will trap Palaxnym and Ith on the other side. We will have no way to reach them, no way I know of."

Voarothim sighed with frustration looking around the cavern with dejected eyes then abruptly he turned back. "Are we sure this is the right cavern and lantern?"

The question was an honest one even if it was a reach beyond any length of one's arm, especially his long limbs. It was evident of that when the look Jura gave him told him so. Her face went slack with incredulity, her eyebrow raised with shock, and even with the Wyrm features of her face he could tell she was numb with disbelief.

"So this is the right cave…and magical lantern?"

"Yes," she said smiling whimsically while shaking her head, "Thaxmosis only has the one lantern in this one cavern."

The Red Dragon coughed into his hand abruptly trying to cover up his wayward question and with a wave of both offered up his plan, "well then, I say we take the lantern and we leave the lair by the quickest egress."

Again, the look he received from Jura was not what he wanted, though expected, now that he was prepared for it. All at once she froze with trepidation, her breathing quickened in contrast, and her yellow eyes locked with his orange ones. "Leave...the lair...to the outside?"

Now, here, would be the true test of her courage Voarothim thought. Here would be the test of her heart and I will not let her do this alone. He nodded and spoke just as calm as he had before to her, reaching past the fear. "Yes, to the outside."

"I do not know if I can leave Voarothim. This place, these caves...Thaxmosis and his cruel will...it is wrong I know but it is all I have ever known."

He picked up the lantern and then her hand, pulling it away from the other stopping the sudden wringing the appendages were doing. She looked deeper into his eyes as he squeezed her hand speaking. "Thaxmosis will know you helped

me Jura. He will know and he will hurt you, maybe even kill you.
You cannot stay here with him...I will not let him hurt you or
Palaxnym or Ith."

The words, each one like a ray of hope, gave her strength
as Jura squeezed back with her hand and whispered. "You will
stay with me once we are outside? You will not leave me?"

Voarothim shook his head quick smiling, "no Jura, I will not
leave you once we are free of this lair."

"The outside, is it..." Jura wanted to ask, her words slowly
fading as she also began to smile with Voarothim.

"Yes, the outside is a world as beautiful as you are Jura
and I will walk with you through it if you will let me."

Oh those sweet words, it was all the Green Dragon needed
to hear to make her final decision. She ran for the exit of the
cavern leading Voarothim away from the cavern and down the
hall to the illusionary façade. As they ran he was careful to hold
the lantern close and wondered if Palaxnym and Ith felt all the
jostling that was happening. The pair moved past the illusionary
wall and out into the alcove without hesitation and then into the
confusion of the passage. A pair Ogres spotted the Dragons and
stopped dead in the hall while staring at them in surprise. Why
would they be hiding in an alcove that goes no-where both

monsters thought?

"Where are we going?" Voarothim asked as they turned and started down the hall away from the Ogres. Just as they did a voice filled with rage screamed at them from further down the passage, the vileness in it causing everyone to stop and some jump.

"JURA! YOU TREACHEROUS WRYM! I WILL HAVE YOUR SKIN AS A RUG FOR WHAT YOU HAVE DONE!"

"Oh no, it is Thaxmosis!" Jura gasped just as Voarothim turned and looked down the passage to see among the throng and mass of guards the taller form of the Great Black Dragon looking at them. "We have to run to the Treasure Chamber, now." She demanded with a jerk of the Red Dragon's hand.

A moment of hesitation finally came, a brief stop as adversaries stared at each other down the long passage. Then one of the Ogres made a move, a quick grab for the robes of the Red Dragon, and met with a boot from Voarothim to the belly. The blow sent the unprepared monster reeling and careening backwards into his counterpart which was enough for the Dragons to escape. Both turned and began to run down the hall, a blur of movement as their magical bodies propelled them along, past unsuspecting guards.

"Why are we going to the Treasure Chamber?" Voarothim asked staying step for step behind Jura.

"Because there is a secret tunnel to the outside in the main room. If we can reach the passage, we might escape!" Jura answered as she knocked over a Northman with her shoulder.

Escape the Terrible One? The strategy seemed built on hope more than practicality Voarothim noted as he kept up, but at this point he would take that hope. Maybe the Terrible One would not chase them once they were free of the lair...maybe?

He flew up the halls of his lair like a whirlwind, the days where his massive wings would generate such a force as to topple trees and raze buildings were gone but Thaxmosis was still a 'Immortalis Lacerta', the Immortal Ones who once ruled this world. He was the Terrible One and just as the name was earned the Great Black Dragon now slammed his way past his own followers and guards. One poor Ogre was pushed with such force as he ran past the monster bounced off the wall and fell to the ground clearly unconscious. The Dragon barely looked back, those drawn to his lair were beneath him and of no concern to Thaxmosis now. He only wanted to find his little Jura and once she was in his hands deliver a punishment which would become legend, a pain so horrendous it would set every soul aghast by its mere mention. Oh my little Green Dragon how I am going to hurt you when I catch you, and catch you I will do. There is no escape from me, the Great Bl-

There she was, her traitorous scent and the young fool Voarothim as well, there they are. Thaxmosis came to a stop at a junction where four halls came to a meet and let his nose guide him. He turned left and knew instantly the pair had come this way just moments ago. They had come from the secret passages he knew, slipped through his lair to his laboratory and destroyed it. The why, as in why the pair had openly defied him, mattered little to the Black Dragon now. No, Thaxmosis only wanted blood and as an Odi ran by his arm shot out and hit the man knocking him into the wall and straight into the dark where he joined the Ogre, unconscious.

There would be copious pain he had decided as he began to run down the passage, a great torrent of torment and agony which she and that churlish Wyrm Voarothim would feel when they were finally under his hand. Oh how the pain would be-

Then, there just ahead in the crowded hall, he spotted them coming out of the break where he kept the magical lantern. Now it made even more sense as to why this was happening and just who had been the true mastermind. That golden, over-righteous minded Dragon had pulled every string and guided his little red imp from afar, it had to be. Voarothim was not capable of infiltrating his lair, so inept was the wyrmling he even had to draw in the clueless Jura to get this far with his plan. Bile, acidic and thick, began to build in his stomach and chest as Thaxmosis screamed with rage at the now fleeing pair.

"JURA! YOU TREACHEROUS WRYM! I WILL HAVE YOUR SKIN AS A RUG FOR WHAT YOU HAVE DONE!"

He watched both turn his direction, eye him with terror, and then spin away and begin to flee again, running away down the passage. One simpleton Ogre tried to grab Voarothim and felt a boot to his stomach for doing such a stupid act. Thaxmosis gave a growl and took off after them screaming for his followers to stop the pair, hold them fast until he arrived, and the Great Black Dragon watched with glee as the fools did just that. Ogres and Trolls began to crowd and stop the pair. Oh the pain h-

For the third time his devious thought was cut short, interrupted, and the nuisance of it all was beginning to make Thaxmosis quite perturbed. He felt someone hit his right shoulder with such force it redirected his sprint and before Thaxmosis could stop the change in course he slammed into the corner of the break which led at one time to the magical lantern he kept in a hidden cavern. It was gone now he knew as his motion came to a thud crunching stop. The Dragon's left shoulder and chest hit the stone wall hard enough to chip the surface and when his eyes stopped shaking Thaxmosis looked up to see the young face of Jared Sinn staring back with a malicious grin and broken mace in his hand.

"I have more questions to ask Terrible One, more inquiries about my past." The newly anointed Paracletus growled.

"I have no more time to answer your questions child," the Dragon hissed like the lizard he was while stepping back out in the passage, brushing off his long robes. "You do not know where your hoard of gold is Paracletus, thus I no longer have a need or a want of you."

"But I have a need of you Thaxmosis," Jared sneered mocking the Dragon as he drew and then spun the swords in his hands, "and you do not have my permission to go till I am done with you!"

The demand, the instruction, was like a slap to Thaxmosis, a mighty blow meant to humble. Yet no one talked like this to the Terrible One, the Great Black Dragon of Thathu. He growled deep feeling the acidic bile in his chest build expanding the inner chamber of his body as it did. Thaxmosis's voice dropped and grumbled as he snarled, "your permission boy? As if I ever would need YOUR PERMISSION FOR ANYTHING!"

It came with a loud roar, a bellow of pure rage that shook the very walls of the lair around them. Jared watched the jaw of Thaxmosis unhinge and drop, like a snakes would do before eating what it had caught for a meal, and then he was running right at the Dragon. Whatever was coming out of the Dragon's mouth Jared was sure it would kill him within the blink of his eye and he surely wanted no part of that. And with just a second to spare he moved clear of a giant spray of black ichor, a thick sticky mucus which coated the floor and adjacent wall where Jared had been standing. Instantly the stone began to hiss as the ichor burned it, the secretion's acidic property melting the rock. The few Trolls and Ogres and Odi who had been unfortunate to be standing close by were struck with small globs of the ichor, splashed with drops of the acid. All began to scream and swipe at the spots trying to push the burning black substance off their bare skin. Even Jared felt the sting of the drops as he rolled by Thaxmosis reaching out and striking the Dragon's leg with his sword as he passed. The metal rang out as if hitting stone and the sting of the acid was joined by the pain humming now in his wrists.

Thaxmosis missed Jared by the slimmest of margins with the strike of his horrific breath attack. The bile was pure acid and he had yet to encounter a substance or material which could resist melting from its touch. Yes, the Great Black Dragon had missed Jared at first, but what the Paracletus did not know was Thaxmosis could draw from an endless supply of the acid and he meant to use as much of it needed to that to kill the young one. He chased the running form of Jared with the spray following just behind the speeding whelp, just missing him with the attack, until he turned and stopped. This round of acidic bile was used up with a small bead of dripping which fell from the lips of Thaxmosis. He stared at Jared and growled with anger, "your luck is impressive young one."

The roll put Jared past the Dragon and as he stood up he took two more steps to lengthen the distance between the two just in case. "And your aim is awful Dragon, how did you get so old? Was it from the generosity of the other Dragons in leaving you be?"

The barb was well thrown and it should have hurt Thaxmosis or at least nicked his ego just a touch, yet the Dragon only grinned with evil. "I told you Jared, I am the wisest creature you will ever meet. I knew the meaning of the carvings in your medallion. I know who you are and where you come from. I know all boy."

"And this wisdom, it helped you live this long life buried in this cave shunning the light of the day?" Jared chuckled still mocking the words of the Dragon.

"Well," Thaxmosis nodded suddenly pointing with one long finger, "it did help me to sense when I was being surrounded."

The remark was a little confusing to Jared, until the hammer blow of a large fist drove into his back and before he knew it he was being shoved down to the floor with one attack after another. He realized a moment to late the Dragon was only toying with him, drawing his attention away so the Trolls and Ogres could attack. He covered his head as more blows rained down, but the last thing he saw of the Dragon was Thaxmosis turning and running down the passage, pursuing something...or someone.

Ten

Rehema, once very long ago, had been called to a meeting at night by the arcane leader of the Thieves Guild of the Unseen Hand, one Kazmir the Rat. It unnerved the Serval to an extreme to be called to a gathering with the master thief. You see, the Guild Master rarely if ever met with any of his council, his 'fingers' you might say, and he never conversed with the low level larceners and pick-pockets under his 'tutelage'. His appearance, as well as his exploits, were a myth which grew and transformed with the seasons with the help of the bards who roamed from pub to pub and from drinking hole to the prostitute's bed. Kazmir was larger than life some whispered, being seven feet tall and as muscled as an Ursi or Equine. Some claimed to have seen him just as he ducked into the shadows of an alley and these souls told the exact opposite, though it was always in low whispered tones so as not to draw looks their way. Kazmir they would smile was barely five-foot-tall and every inch as diabolical. The Rat had stolen anything and everything in the city of Thesedell at least once the stories told, from gems to magical items, and according to some he stole *the articles a second and even a third time just to prove there was nothing he could not take or touch. Oh yes, the Master Thief and Guild Master was untouchable, enigmatic...and he had called her to a secret meeting.*

She walked into a small room at the back of some abandoned building on the lower end of the city where the dregs and the forgotten lived, nervous and yet unflustered she entered. If she had to meet this mystery that was Kazmir then she would at least act like a capable thief. There was nothing in the room with the exception of a table in the center and a scattering of candles to provide light. She was led in by the same human who had given them the orders to fetch the Eye of the Moon from the treasure chamber, Scars. How he had come by the name no one was sure, he was quite handsome without a mark on his face Rehema thought for a human. Scars was Kazmir's left hand, not the right which most would see coming, but the left which was always hidden from sight. She had heard once on the street he was a 'reformed' member of the Red Blades but that could never be the truth. No one left the Red Blades, or the Remnants as they were called now, at least not alive and of their own choice. Rehema nodded when Scars motioned for her to enter the room and then froze when his cold eyes locked to hers and he told her with no emotion if she mentioned this meeting to anyone he would find out and then kill both her and whoever she spoke to, very badly. It was the threat, and the cold look of those eyes, which caused her to listen carefully to ensure he had left the room when the door closed. The thought of Scars being behind her unsettled Rehema even more than she was already.

"Do not worry little kitten, the bad man is gone." A voice called from the shadows, common and yet dignified.

"I know, but you will allow me the courtesy of checking?" She asked back to the dark.

"No please," the voice answered and she could almost picture the smile on a face as it spoke, "by all means go and take a look."

So she did, slowly and purposefully ensuring the 'bad man' was gone from the small room. Then she turned back and there he was, the infamous Master Thief to some and the extraordinary Guild Master to others, and he played the role of mysterious leader to the hilt. He was dressed as a commoner in simple leathers and a coat, a pair of mid-calf boots which had seen better days filled out the ruse perfectly. This is Kazmir Rehema thought, the one we all strive to knock from the mountain top in the guild. Oh it was him. She could tell because his eyes cut straight to her soul like a knife. They were not beady or small, but full yellow with a dark iris. His face was like a Rat complete with small whiskers, his body covered in the small white fur of his kind where it showed. His hands were small but strong looking, the wrists of both arms adorned with plain rope bracelets.

"What do you wish of me, a simple thief in your guild, my master?"

"And how do you know I am the Guild Master little kitten?"

The Serval gave a small shake of her head while never once breaking eye contact, falling just a little into his eyes. "I just know. My instincts tell me so."

"Instincts, now there is an edge every good thief must have, much more than a trusted lock pick or a favorite dagger." Kazmir smiled, not fatherly but like a long lost lover. The expression drew a shiver down Rehema's back as she nodded, not out of fear but something else.

"That is true, but those are words a master thief would remind a lowly pickpocket of while teaching. Is that why I am here my Guild Master, to be taught?"

Kazmir only smiled and replied with a puzzle and a wave of his hand to the shadows at the edge of the room. "My need of you is, let us say, a prolonged one Rehema. For now, I simply need you to stand back in the shadows and observe."

She looked to the shadows hesitating for just a moment.

She was already in too deep to back away now, and she was not sure she would if given the chance, so Rehema stepped quietly into the dark of the shadows and stood there just as quiet as instructed. She turned to see Kazmir was busy doing something to his face, rubbing it with the palms of his hands it looked like, and it was only when he stopped and she saw the change did she realize he was disguising his features. Gone was the look of the Rat, replaced by an old burrower, a close enough visage to a weasel no one would think twice. Rehema inhaled deeply as the shock of seeing how fast the Guild Master had changed his appearance set in just before a sudden noise broke the silence.

A single knock rang in the room which drew her eyes to the door. A second two-quick knock on the table top came in reply from Kazmir and the door opened instantly. Rehema slowed her breathing so as not to give away her hiding place in the dark while Scars led in a Simian, a very well dressed one at that. He's someone very important, the expensive leathers and condescending attitude gave the fact away. When the Simian crossed the floor going face to face with Kazmir in his disguise she was sure Scars would kill the Chimp. No one would dare, could try and approach the Guild Master in such a fashion, not even a lord or a king. And yet, Kazmir only stood and watched calmly as the Simian growled.

Where is my wife and daughter? He asked bringing up a finger and pointing menacingly at Kazmir.

The Rat only smiled clam, just as he had done with her, and told the Simian to get himself under control. Unleashing his anger at the one, the only one, who could help would only make a dire matter worse and no one wanted that. The Simian heard the creak of leather from behind and slowly turned, just as she had done, to find Scars with his hand on the handle of a rather insidious looking hand axe. As the Simian began to understand where he was and who he was dealing with he turned and asked Kazmir where his wife and daughter were again, only in a more uncertain and lower tone. The bluster and anger from before, born of a desperation she had never experienced and never wanted too, was lost to fear. Where are they the Simian begged, he would pay any amount to have them returned.

Rehema had no clue to what game Kazmir was playing and at the moment she did not care, so drawn in by the actions of the Simian. What had happened to his wife and daughter she wanted to know, needed to know suddenly she thought as Kazmir took over the conversation and the room with practiced ease. How much would you pay the Rat asked? How much are the most precious things in your life worth to you? Tell me, is there even an amount one could dream of for such a prize?

Why do you ask such a thing sir? The Simian stammered, that fear in his heart growing at the ominous question. Rehema felt it blooming into hers as well now as the Rat cocked his head to the side and spoke.

I am just an old weasel, a burrower from the mountains, but even I know everything has a price my friend. Sometimes that price is gold and sometimes, for some people, that price is something else more precious than gold or silver. You are close to the ones who rule the Southland, the Pans, right?

The Simian's eyes narrowed as he slowly nodded. Yes, my uncle and my wife's brother are advisors to the ones who rule. Why, what does that have to do with my wife and daughter being kidnapped? Did someone take them hoping I would influence our leader?

No, influence is not the same as blood Kazmir responded and the remark left the Simian confused as he stared back.

Yes, what does that have to do with this Rehema asked silently as Kazmir stepped back and spoke altering the ground under everyone's feet. Your wife and daughter are safe sir, both at this moment are being ushered into the Royal Keep at the center of Thesedell by the guards and the ones who look after the Pride and Pack. Kazmir the Rat freed them from their kidnappers while you were being brought here and delivered them to safety, after disposing of the abductors of course. The Lions and Mastiffs who rule the city will ensure both are taken care of until you arrive.

The Chimpanzee gasped at the news, the abruptness of it hitting him square in the chest. The Simian's legs, weakened by the news, began to give and if not for Kazmir grabbing the arm of the Chimp he might have fallen to the floor. Are you sure of this? You are not saying such a thing to make me pay some ransom?

Why would I want a ransom? I do not have your wife and daughter, now or ever, and what amount would I ask for since we have already determined there is no reasonable price I could ask for the Rat chuckled.

But this one called Kazmir, why would he do this...for someone he does not know? The Simian asked getting himself under control, straightening his vest and clothes.

Because, the Rat stated with a smile, no one comes to Thesedell and works the streets without paying Kazmir. The ones who took your family, they broke the one rule which thieves must never break, and that is never disrespect the Guild Master.

The Chimpanzee stared at the Rat for a moment as the last set off the flashes of recognition in his mind. He sighed and spoke as someone who understood once again where and who he was dealing with. Then I am to owe this Kazmir for my family's return the Simian asked rhetorically, the answer already in his mind. The Rat only smiled, he knew the Chimp was quite aware of the situation and had no need of words. As the Simian left to leave, and Rehema began to breathe again, he stopped short at the door abruptly and turned back. Which one was it, my uncle or her brother? Which one perpetrated this horrible act? He asked with a stern tone.

When you return home to Grand Simian city of Gobara, there will be one there to greet you and one who will not be Kazmir answered, and there was nothing more to the cryptic statement because there was no need. The Simian understood, the remark about blood now fully realized, and left without so much as a glance back and as he left the room Rehema stepped out of the shadows as Kazmir removed his disguise. "You saved his family to obtain a favor?" She asked looking to him with a curious expression.

"No," Kazmir remarked walking up to her, "I left a message for others in this city that I will not be disregarded or disrespected. You want to work in my city, you pay my toll to be here."

It could have been that easy, that simple, but Rehema knew better as she shook her head. "No, I think you did it to get a favor for when you need it."

"Your instincts tell you this little kitten?"

"No," Rehema remarked this time as the Rat walked past her to the door, "it's the play a master thief would make, the same one Kazmir the Rat would make."

He stopped and looked back smiling again, "then tell me, what else did you learn tonight?"

"To never let a situation slip away from you, to always be in control from the beginning." She answered and when the Rat winked she felt a touch of pride.

"Good instincts, follow them always kitten."

Why, at this moment when she was at death's proverbial door, did she remember that first of many meeting with the Guild Master. It was simple, she screamed at herself as the bugs came at them, this situation had slipped right out of her hands which you never let happen. If they had stuck together, the humans and the Anthros, then they might have taken the bugs easily. Yet the twins broke for the entrance to the chamber screaming like banshees while Elas and Lalya chose to stand and fight charging at the enlarged vermin.

Damn, we split right down the middle.

And then Rolft screamed again running away from the exit

he had sought so desperately just moments before. As he did the entry filled with the bodies of Ogres and Trolls and Odi.

Now we are in some serious trouble Rehema thought as she drew her sword and readied her arm for the work ahead.

"Someone just knocked Thaxmosis down!"

The words from Voarothim barely registered in the mind of Jura as she ran down the hall avoiding guards, sometimes with a side step and sometimes with a shoulder, but enough of his statement caught her attention. She turned to look back as she held her long robes up with one hand and watched as a being rose just in front of the Great Black Dragon, who looked angrier than she had ever seen him before. The Green Dragon spun back turning to run on while she pulled her new friend harder, spurring her legs to move faster.

"I think it was the Paracletus, the one from before...Jared was his name, I think?"

She growled low and yelled choosing not to look back at the moment, "can you pick a better time to ask me that question, preferably when we are not being chased by an Ancient Dragon?"

"Oh, I see your point, look out!" Voarothim pointed out just as a female Odi stepped out from an alcove. She barely had a chance to turn and catch sight of Jura just as the Dragon knocked her down before disappearing down the passage, yet not without asking for forgiveness.

"I am sorry. I hope you will be fine!"

The pair followed the specific route Jura told Rehema and the thieves to follow, step for step traveling down the same passages and when coming to the fork darting down the correct tunnel. Jura had seen the young Paracletus confront and in the process stop Thaxmosis which meant they had a small chance now of staying alive now. Just moments before she was sure she and Voarothim would be caught, skinned alive, and served to the Howler for an evening meal, only the Paracletus Jared had given them a gift. A precious present of time, just a mere trickle of sand in the hour glass, but time nonetheless and Jura wanted to waste not one bit of the advantage they had gained. She pulled the Red Dragon along with her mad dash easily navigating the twists and turns and bumps of the tunnel leading to the treasure chamber, but all did not end as happy as she wanted or hoped.

There was one last turn, a sharp one to the right, and then maybe four steps before one entered the massive treasure chambers of the Great Black Dragon. Jura was sure there was no one to block their entrance into the main cavern, so sure she was that the Green Dragon failed to hear the sounds of battle. So intent was Jura on making their escape that she failed to see the lone Odi standing in the entryway, a bow in his hand with the string taught and arrow nocked ready for flight. The human looked over just in time to see the seven-foot Dragon barreling toward him and let out a scream. Jura never made a sound, not a one except when she hit the Odi and knocked him and his bow into the cavern unceremoniously. The human's arrow, whom he had been aiming at now a mystery, flew with a straightness right into an unaware Troll Shaman's leg. All at once the monster's chanting came to an end, exchanged with a loud bellow of pain as the missile sank deep into its fleshy thigh.

"Yahhhhh!"

The Odi, no longer a combatant, became a sudden speed decelerator as he fell to the ground before getting entangled in the legs of Jura. The Green Dragon let go of Voarothim, or tried too, as she fell to the ground, only with momentum working against her the attempt at a save failed as she fell on her side. With a loud 'oof' the Red Dragon landed across both Jura and the now incapacitated Odi along with losing the lantern, the vessel skidding across the floor and ending up well away from him. The heap that was two Dragons and a human garnered little attention from the others in the chamber as the combatants went to work attacking each other.

Elas let out a yell and charged into the battle going right for a spider as it skittered with its eight long legs toward him and Lalya. The bug tried to draw first blood with a lunge rush snapping its fangs at the canine and trying to grab him with two of its front legs. Elas dodged the assault though with ease stepping back while swinging his short sword with a snap of his back hand. The blow was not meant to kill only hurt and when the blade slashed across the spider's fangs the vermin stopped momentarily, long enough for the Canine to counter with an upward cut to one of the insect's legs. Unlike the slash with his back hand this cut was meant to draw more than blood. Elas had every intent to sever the leg with one mighty hack, only the sword hit the limb and bounced off with a loud clang. The spider's shell was tougher than he assumed Elas thought as the vermin charged in again but came to a sudden stop when a small dart flew in and struck true, right into one of its many eyes. A howling screech went up from the insect as it skittered backwards now, retreating from the fight so fast it threw gold coins and gems in every direction from the mound of treasure it was on.

The dart was from the hand crossbow of Lalya Elas knew and that was as much as he could deduce because one of the beetles took the place of the spider with a blink of his large eyes. He barely leapt backwards away from the vermin as it attacked, strange mandibles in a foreign looking head clicking in an attempt to grab him. He slashed downward with his sword slamming the blade into what he thought was the bug's head and just like the spider's leg his weapon bounced off with no damage visible. The Canine continued to back pedal to get away as the vermin kept up its pursuit of him.

She watched her friend trying to flee the beetle while reloading her hand crossbow. Lalya was suddenly struck with the memory of a secret promise she agreed to with Elas's lover, Drax the Puma. She had promised to return the Canine unharmed to his lover's embrace and look now, she might falter and fail on that pledge. Lalya's hands moved with rapid precision as she loaded her weapon while she watched her friend dance away from the beetle again as his sword failed to penetrate the bug's hard carapace. She brought the crossbow up just as her friend jumped up to elude another lunge by the giant beetle, Elas's feet landing deftly on top of the bug's back. He ran then off its back to its rear disappearing behind a mound of gold coins and treasure.

"Hah!" Lalya screamed giving a cry of triumph just as one of the twin brothers yelled about a Troll. She turned to see the large green monster running toward her, an evil intent on its large face. Well, I have to shoot something she thought grinning and firing her crossbow bolt straight into the knee of the Troll with a loud hiss and abrupt crack of bone breaking.

The Troll screamed in pain and dropped to its hands and knees, a defenseless position which Lalya took advantage of. Before the Troll could react she drew her short sword, the end curved like a Simian's scimitar, and with a vicious cut relieved the monster of its head. As the large bulbous skull rolled across the floor the Fox growled, 'come back from that Troll!"

There was no time to enjoy the small victory as the sound of gold being scattered caught the Fox's ear and she turned in time to see the spider she had shot with her crossbow earlier charging her. Lalya barely had time to block a strike of the bug's leg and then a second attack so there was no chance to reload her crossbow. She backpedaled just as Elas had done to increase the distance between her and the spider only the bug had no intention to let its prey escape. It lunged again and this time Lalya barely blocked its fangs from sinking deep into body with a hard slap from the flat of her blade. The spider stepped back from the blow and then a dagger hit its side with a loud pop as the dart broke skin. The bug shrieked for a second time skittering away to seek safety once again but now Lalya gave chase, the tables had turned in her favor and she was now the one who refused to let her prey get away. She ran at the fleeing bug then came to a skidding stop as a large spear flew right past her head missing her by the smallest of measurements. She looked up to see an Ogre scream a battle cry and run at her.

"Oh damn, damn, damn…"

The Fox scampered back down the mound to find Rehema driving her sword into the back of the body of the same spider she and Elas had been trying to kill just moments before. Lalya watched as the spider shrieked one last time from the thief's deadly backstab, its legs jutting outward as it collapsed dead. The Serval yanked her sword free just as Lalya ran up yelling. "We have to get out of here, reinforcements just arrived!"

"The Troll Shaman called for other guards?" Rehema called back while hopping off the bug's body.

"I do not know, but there are others here now!" Lalya answered just as the Ogre rounded the mound of treasure. Each hand held a large stout club of wood, like small trees, and the monster meant to use both on Lalya and Rehema.

"Find Elas and then try and find a way out of here!" The Serval ordered as she jumped away from Lalya.

"I can do that!" Lalya shouted back breaking in the other direction. The move left the Ogre confused for a moment, which way was he supposed to go? Which Anthro was he supposed to kill first, the Cat or the Fox? It stood for a moment looking back and forth between the two wandering what to do before running after the Serval.

The thieves had survived the bugs and now the Trolls and Ogres, but then someone new entered the massive chambers and the fight changed instantly.

Eleven

———————●———————

When he fell, Voarothim lost his perspective of the area instantly as the world turned upside down in a blink. One moment he was standing and running and the next he was partially on top of Jura watching the lantern, the magical vessel which contained Palaxnym and Ith, bounce and spin away from his outstretched arm and hand. He did not see the battle erupting around him until the Troll Shaman screamed and then the clash and clang of weapons striking against each other reached his ears. The Red Dragon looked up just as a giant scorpion chased a human, one of the twins, from the library across the chamber. He had to take a quick double take to ensure he was seeing exactly what he was seeing and as Voarothim's mind was agreeing with his eyes that yes, that was a large scorpion chasing a human from the library, Jura pushed him while grunting loudly.

"Get up Voarothim! We have to flee with the lantern!"

The Red Dragon rolled awkwardly off the small pile of legs and arms looking back to see the Odi they had landed on was quite unconscious. Voarothim stood up and helped Jura just as one of the Trolls in the battle turned and spotted the pair. The monster stared at them then looked down to see the magical lantern on the floor before turning its attention back to them. "What are you two doing with that?"

Jura opened her mouth to respond and suddenly was without words, being confronted striking her numb for some silly reason. Voarothim looked to her then back to the Troll and was about to answer when a human, not one of the twins, slashed an Ogre across its ample belly with a quick counter to the brute's attack which stopped him. The human charged the Troll then who had confronted them with a scream and the monster accepted the challenge with its own war cry and charge. Voarothim leaned back and spoke to Jura without looking to her for a moment, "I think we can leave now."

"Yes, that would be the best thing to do." She replied quietly as the pair began to move with a slow but intended purpose toward the lantern. The fight was in full effect all around them, the vermin and monsters attacking the Anthros and humans with abandon. A small bolt flew between them from somewhere and Jura gave a small jerk from surprise while Voarothim did the same added with a mumbled curse. The Dragons moved quicker then stopping only once to let an Ogre run past chasing someone, who they were not sure. Both only had one thing in mind and that was retrieving the lantern and making an escape and when they reached the vessel Voarothim quickly bent down and picked it up smiling proudly.

"I have it!"

Jura smiled just as brightly with relief ready to tell him the secret tunnel was just in the rear of this chamber, a short distance to run. Only she never had the chance to tell him anything of the sort. A loud scream drew almost everyone's attention to the entrance to the chamber.

"HERE, THE WAY OUT IS CLEAR!" Rolft screamed for his companions to hear and hopefully follow as he ran to the entrance. He spotted his brother Fendrel and Baldric, both looking to him, as well as the Cat Rehema, but the other two Anthros were fighting somewhere else in the treasure chamber. Those two are on their own Rolft started to think before being cut short as something thick and viscous spewed from down the tunnel covering him from his head to his feet. It was not moment later that the searing pain struck Rolft, like being set on fire, and he let out a second bellowing howl of pain as his skin began to bubble and burn.

"Oh no, no, no…" Jura whispered over and over as she immediately recognized the ichor which covered the human. It was Thaxmosis and his acid...and now the poor human would suffer a horrible death.

Rehema stood atop the treasure mound watching in horror, speechless, as the human thief Rolft was sprayed in some black tar like liquid. She gasped and stepped back when the man screamed in pure agony and began to tear at his own skin and body. He's melting her mind yelled over and over, melting and dissolving into a red and black puddle. She could only watch in that same horror as Rolft's body literally fell apart, legs breaking as the bones weakened and snapped while his arms fell free from softened and disintegrating shoulder sockets. And all the while Rolft screamed and screamed until there was just a final gurgle of a cry, the last human sound he could make before crumbling into a pile of still dissolving bits and parts.

"BROTHER!" Fendrel screamed, the pain and shock at the sight of his twin's death far too easy to hear in his voice. He started forward with a small step when someone filled the entire entrance to the chamber. A tall form, dark and malevolent, appeared in the door and the fear in the room was suddenly so deep and drowning, swallowing anyone and all looking at the one standing in the entrance to the chamber.

He heard the sounds of the fighting long before he reached his precious treasure chamber and this incensed Thaxmosis even more than he already was, it infuriated him. Thieves, or larceners or whatever you wish to call them, had dared to slither into his lair like slugs and that was evil enough but now those same pilferers had dared to find and enter his treasure chamber, to steal his beloved hoard of gold. There would be no mercy the Great Black Dragon of Thathu had decided, no charity given to the thieves once he caught them and he would catch them. So when he saw the human standing there in the entrance to his treasure chamber screaming for the others of his kind to follow, well, Thaxmosis made sure the chance to flee would no longer be a choice.

With a great spray he covered the human with his acidic bile and then watched with a smile as the fool melted on the spot. Then he stepped into the entryway and looked out into the chamber feeling dismay at first, pure shock at the violation of his sanctum by these…thieves. The Great Black Dragon looked from eye to eye feeling his rage and fury blossom and rise in his heart and mind. With each deep inhale he took his anger exploded and with each exhale he let his malevolence flow outward spreading through the chamber like an invisible fog. He watched as each intruder suddenly felt the evil that was Thaxmosis flow over them, how each began to find it hard to breath and move. Even his followers and the giant bugs were unable to move, unable to look away. They were all terrified to the very center of their beings, frozen with fear to their cores. He inhaled deeply, his chest expanding as he did, and then with a bellow the Dragon let all know their fate.

"No one will leave this chamber alive...YOU ALL WILL DIE!"

Rehema blinked as her body began to tremble from the sight of the Dragon, his presence. Her mother had told her once many years ago a story about how when she was a little kitten she had come across a being which had scared her so much she could not move or think. What was it little Rehema had whispered? Her mother only shook her head and sighed, I do not know my little one but it was old, so very old. How do you know that mother? Because kitten, when evil is allowed to linger and live for so many years its power grows and its presence becomes a shadow which covers the soul and takes the light from it. At the time she failed to understand what her mother was trying to say but now, here with the Ancient Dragon in the chamber, Rehema understood. Oh, the dark shroud this one cast was long and it stole the light from everything it touched her mind stammered. She was frozen to the spot on the pile of treasure staring at the Dragon when it turned and looked to the one called Jura and snarled.

"You, betrayer, I will eat you alive and suck the marrow from your bones!"

The Serval watched with distant eyes as the Green Dragon tried to respond to the threat, to her former master, but nothing came out when her mouth moved. So struck by the Ancient Dragon's shadow Jura could not respond, but the one next to her could. With a surprise shift, a small move, Voarothim stood tall to this threat by slowly sliding forward taking Thaxmosis and his attention full on. "I will not let you harm her Terrible One."

If one expected a sharp verbal retort, and there had to be a counter to this brave and defiant act, then one would be shocked even more when the Great Black Dragon of Thathu did not give one. Thaxmosis simply growled at the Red Dragon, low and menacing, and then in a blink which no one could follow he crossed the chamber and effortlessly snatched Voarothim up with a single hand to the throat, lifting the Dragon free of the ground so his feet dangled in the air while the lantern the young Dragon was holding flew across the chamber landing off by another pile of gold. Thaxmosis tightened his grip, a sick cracking sound coming from his hand as the Red Dragon's scales began to pop from the pressure.

"You dare challenge me Voarothim! Your scales are thin, your claws are dull, and your fire weak little Wyrm. I am Ancient and-"

"Let him go!" A voice demanded cutting him off. Thaxmosis, still holding Voarothim high, turned to see Jura glaring at him as she growled again. "Let him go, now!"

"Patience Jura, I will come to you shortly," the Great Black Dragon hissed back.

"Then in death I will finally be free of you Thaxmosis, but not before I see you let go of Voarothim, NOW!" The Green Dragon screamed.

There was no response from the Terrible One, no words. Only the hard hateful glare as he turned toward her while still holding Voarothim free of the floor with the one arm. His deep breaths were like the sounds a bellows makes when a smithy stokes the flames of his forge, only the forge here was the chest of the Great Black Dragon. His mouth opened slowly and Rehema was sure he would spew the acid again, cover Jura with it, and yet the Green Dragon stood her ground defiant and strong.

"LET HIM GO!" She demanded with the force of her scream, but the only answer she received almost immediately was one she did not want to hear.

"No,"

Just as Thaxmosis had done moments ago when he crossed the chamber to grab Voarothim in a blink of an eye so did Jura use all the might of her Dragon lineage to do the same. Lalya, standing across the cavern, barely saw the sudden move Jura made. It was a blur, the loud crack of a slap, and then she was looking at this new Dragon now holding both of the smaller ones. He still had the red one by the throat and now the green one by the wrist of her hand. Thaxmosis saw the attack long before Jura was close enough to strike and with ease he caught her wrist in mid-swing, just a breath before squeezing the limb...hard. He grinned with evil as she gasped in pain and dropped to her knee while reaching up to free her arm.

"You will always belong to me Jura...always!" Thaxmosis hissed and as the Green Dragon looked up into his eyes with fear he smiled more. He was the master here in his lair. He bestowed life and he took it away when he deemed. No one, Anthro or Dragon or Human or Monster was his equal, no one!

And then something moving with the amazing speed of a Dragon flew into the chamber from the entrance and struck the Terrible One like a battering ram, a full on smash sending both combatants further back into the chamber and away from Jura and Voarothim. The young Dragons fell to the ground, being abruptly freed leaving them off balance, just as a loud scream erupted in the chamber.

Jared finished off the last Ogre with a strike from the flat side of his sword and then was in full pursuit of Thaxmosis within moments of losing sight of the Dragon. It was not hard to follow the path the Terrible One took, all you had to do was look for the scattered guards, most knocked to the floor while a few were left leaning on the walls of the underground lair. He ran as fast as his legs could propel him moving just like the Dragons, so quick eyes could not follow. The guards in the halls felt a gust of wind and then nothing as Jared bolted past all till he came to a skidding stop in the middle of the passage, right in front of a door with a strange symbol. It's the door to the treasure chamber of Thaxmosis, his sanctuary someone had said. Jared wasted no more time than it took to step through the portal and begin to descend the long stairway in leaps. He was not sure how he knew this was the way to find the Great Black Dragon, he just did and Jared ran full out once he reached the end of the steps. He also was not sure why he was chasing the Dragon. He had his answers, somewhat, so why pursue a creature which might kill him?

Because something inside Jared told him too...that he had too.

He had pushed the news of his father, if it was true, out of his mind. Jared concentrated on each step he landed on and when his boots hit level ground he pressed his legs harder, running even faster. He had no time to think, if it were true, if his father had killed his mother...had hilled all those innocent people at Pallator? No, there was nothing in his mind about his past, just the next step and what he might have to do when he finally found the Great Black Dragon. Suddenly the fork in the tunnel was on him and Jared just let his instincts take over, let his churning legs chose which new tunnel to run down. Then he was down this new path and he let his mind think of one other thing beside the pursuit.

What to do when he found Thaxmosis.

He had weapons but the hide of the Dragon would be tough, as thick as the steel in his hands. Jared squeezed the sword grips in his right and left hand as he ran. Please, let me have picked the right tunnel his mind pleaded and when the passage broke hard right up ahead Jared heard the sound of the battle.

Yes, the right path he smiled as he navigated the turn and then he saw the entrance to the treasure chamber. He pushed his legs yet again as Jared burst from the entrance into the low light of the cavern. All around him Anthros and Humans were fighting

Monsters and Odi, and then just up ahead Jared saw Thaxmosis, both of the Dragons held firmly in his hands. Now he knew why he had chased after the Terrible One, why he pursued certain death. A sense of protecting, so strong and unbreakable, surged through Jared lending a sudden rush of power to his muscles. With a mighty leap he hurtled his large frame at the Great Black Dragon meaning to run him over using his shoulder and legs, and Jared might have if not at the last moment Thaxmosis had not let go of the Wyrms and turned his attention to the attacking Paracletus.

Still, when Jared hit Thaxmosis, slamming into him and driving him backwards, it was like hitting a mountain the young Paracletus thought.

Twelve

When the young Paracletus hit the larger Thaxmosis the sound was like stone hitting stone, a loud crack that reverberated through the chamber. Elas jerked and shook his head as his sensitive ears hurt from the sound. He breathed deep as he watched incredulously, that young Anthro actually took the tall Dragon for a short ride, that was until the Dragon stopped the assault after being pushed only a few steps. Then he gasped again as he watched the smaller form of the Anthro get tossed to the back of the chamber, thrown like he was nothing more than a sack of river rocks. There was a loud crash from somewhere back there in the rear of the chamber, but Elas had no time to ponder if the young Anthro was alive after being thrown such a distance. The beetle from before had turned around and was coming for him again, its mandibles clicking along with each of its legs.

"Damn," the Canine hissed sidestepping away from the giant bug. He had no choice but to flee, he had not a single weapon capable of cracking the beetle's hard shell. He might have brought along an axe if he had known they would end up fighting giant bugs!

He jumped to the bottom of the pile just as the bug tried to catch him with its mandibles and then with a quick turn Elas spun and struck the beetle with a hard slash. The blow, once again, only met the hard carapace of the beetle and bounced off, but this time because of the downward position the bug was at the strike knocked it off balance. Before the beetle could react it fell, tumbled down the pile of coins, and landed flat on the floor of the cavern...upside down. Its legs began to churn and kick as the bug desperately tried to right itself only Elas would not let that happen. The Canine jumped in and plunged his sword right through the bugs throat, or what he guessed was its throat, feeling the blade tip hit the cavern floor with a clang and a bone jarring 'hum' in his hands. The bug gave a shrieking cry, its legs churning harder for a moment, as if it had every intention of still getting up. Elas gave his blade a hard twist and this time the beetle finally succumbed to death. Its legs stopped moving mercifully.

Elas stood up yanking his sword from the dead bug's body and turned. The fight was still raging. The reinforcements were still coming for the thieves as well as the bugs. There was no time to rest as the Canine jumped back into the fight, or more like pushed because a Troll was coming to finish what the beetle could not. He growled low and menacing causing the Monster to pause and Elas took advantage of the hesitation by lunging and slashing at the Troll with a loud yell.

Lalya fired another bolt from her hand crossbow watching as it struck one of the last Odi clean in his shoulder knocking the human to the ground. She hooked the weapon back on her belt quickly after firing her last dart. She was out of bolts which left her with just the short sword in her left hand and the dagger on her hip. The Fox pulled her dagger free from its sheath just as a familiar yell brought her attention round, straight to Elas as he attacked the Troll. She wasted little time and bolted to help her friend watching as the Canine slashed the monster deep across its chest before slipping to the right, escaping a slash from the Troll's clawed hand. Lalya let out her own cry as she leapt to the fray catching the monster looking toward Elas and not her. She hacked the monster with her sword across its arm feeling the blade hit bone with a crunch and yet amazingly as Lalya jumped away to avoid a counter she noted the Troll was not bleeding, not a single drop. Its power to regenerate already healing its body from the damage the pair of thieves had delivered.

"We have to cut off its head!" Elas screamed lunging in

and hacking the Troll across its back with a heavy blow when it turned to Lalya. The monster cried out in its guttural language and spun throwing a backhand at the Canine, who ducked the blow easily.

"I know what we have to do Elas!" The Fox retorted as she made a mighty cut to the monster's exposed leg when it looked to Elas. The blow was deep, to the bone yet again, and this time it hobbled the monster. The Troll fell to one knee, the leg Lalya had cut, and one hand keeping its body off the treasure pile. The monster was hurt, down, but it would not stay that way and both the thieves knew this as fact. Lalya and Elas both began to stab and hack at the monster removing its upraised arm which it was using to try and hold the attackers back. Then Elas saw his chance to remove the Troll's head and end this fight and he moved to deliver one final cut to the monster's neck. Yet before he was able to end the Troll's life something struck his chest with enough force to knock him backwards down onto the pile of coins with a loud thud.

"Elas!" Lalya cried out as her friend fell. It was an arrow, from behind her mind screamed as the Fox turned with a snap to see where and who was aiming at the Canine. She spotted the Odi immediately, the same one she had shot with her last bolt. The human had somehow gathered himself and loosed an arrow…at her. Damn that man, he missed me and struck my friend.

"Elas!" The Fox screamed the name again as she watched the Odi nock another arrow and begin to draw back the string of his bow. The sound of coins rolling down the pile broke the stare the Fox was giving the Odi and she turned to see the large scorpion speeding toward her and Elas. We are easy prey now she thought while backpedaling away from the bug as it pursued her, and to just add a little more 'tension' to the predicament she found herself in, Lalya noticed the Troll was healed enough now to gain his feet.

"Get up Elas!" She screamed turning full round and running for the Canine. She could hear the scorpion scurrying toward her faster, the Troll growling as it began its chase of her, and Lalya was sure the Odi was going to shoot her in the back any moment now. Only the scorpion and the Troll never reached her and the Odi, well he never took the shot. All the Fox knew was she made the side of Elas, who had rolled over onto his stomach, and dropped down beside him.

"How bad are you hurt?"

"My chest…the arrow did not break my armor but I am not so sure of my bones." The Canine gasped in pain.

Lalya smiled unable to contain her relief for her friend

being alive, for not having to tell Drax his love was dead. "We need to get moving my friend or we will both be dead."

A screech cut off Elas before he could respond and when he rolled back over enough he could see the scorpion was almost to them, its claws snipping wildly, eagerly. This is not how he was supposed to meet his end the Dae thought fighting back the newly developed pain of breathing.

The Odi with the bow gave a shrill whistling gasp as Baldric's dagger slipped between his ribs, up to the hilt, and punctured his insides. The human turned to look into to the cold eyes of the thief/assassin as his life ebbed away with the last two beats of his heart. There was no compassion in those eyes, no sorrow or apprehension. There was just cruel indifference.

"She is mine Odi, mine to kill…"

Baldric let the human fall to the ground in a lump as he squatted low keeping his profile the same to the room. He had the advantage, no one was looking for him, be it bug or monster or even his own companions. Baldric was a memory to the ones he came in with, a ghost in the battle here in the cavern, and that would be everyone's undoing. When the fighting started he took to shadows leaving the others to face the enemies. Baldric still had to fulfill the task set out by the head of the Red Remnant, the Serval and her companions were not to return to Thesedell. 'Dispatch them Baldric, all three, and your entry to the Red Remnant will be assured' Drezek told him. The man was the right hand of the Master Assassin of the guild, why would he lie? And anyway, Baldric hated that little kitten and he would certainly enjoy watching her die, feeling her last heartbeat through his dagger's blade. He scanned the cavern and the battle quickly spotting the Serval as she ran down a large pile of coins toward the two young Dragons who were trying to get up off the ground. The thief/assassin squinted and started to move, circling round using the shadows to keep out of the line of anyone's sight and thus out of the battle. His plan was to get behind the Serval and the Dragons taking all three by surprise. Baldric was sure he could get Rehema in his attack and from the intentions of the owner of this lair and treasure, the Ancient Dragon would take care of everyone else. A scream drew a quick look and check to his right as the thief/assassin watched the Fox and the Canine slide and roll down a large pile of gold fleeing the large scorpion. Then to his left Fendrel charged two of the Ogre's with a loud war cry, foolish thing for a thief to do, but then the remaining twin was never the smartest of the pair.

Well, maybe the Ancient Dragon will have three less to rid

his domain of Baldric thought as he moved into position behind the trio. It would certainly be a help to him the thief/assassin thought. Rehema did not see him either as he squatted lower in the dark getting ready to strike at the Cat.

For a moment, maybe longer, the world spun as Jared fought to keep his wits about him. The Terrible One was stronger, stouter, then the young Paracletus was expecting and ready for. Jared had growled before hitting Thaxmosis fully intending to drive the Dragon across the cavern, and then the growl turned into a grunt when he hit the rock hard body. His legs kept driving, pushing the Great Black Dragon backwards, but then Thaxmosis dug his clawed feet into the ground and Jared suddenly was unable to move the body another step. His legs gave out with a second grunt, and with the help of an arm across his back Jared went to a knee with the air in his lungs leaving in a great rush. Damn, he thought through the pain, I almost had him. Then Jared was flying, the ground and piles of treasure speeding by beneath him as he crossed the cavern through the air. Hopefully the landing will not be so bad Jared thought as a large pile of gold coins and jewelry appeared abruptly, a moment before he hit it square with a loud crash.

The landing was...well, it was quite uncomfortable.

Thaxmosis growled loud in triumph as he watched the halfwit Paracletus end up somewhere deeper inside his treasure chamber. He was about to turn back toward the betrayers Jura and Voarothim when one of the human thieves came at him screaming, some inane babble about his brother being killed. The Great Black Dragon only snarled and cut the poor thief clean in two almost with a slash of his hand and claws, the human falling at his feet with a dying cry. Imbeciles all, knaves and boors, and all will meet the same fate Thaxmosis had decided as he slowly turned and looked to see two had become three and all were now farther away fidgeting with his magical lantern.

The Serval Cat knew they were in a perilous and dire situation. Her and her friends could have escaped the Odi and Monsters with more than a fair chance but now, with an Ancient Dragon attacking, there was little chance she and her friends would see the light of a new day. Rehema struck at the last of the beetles knocking away its mandibles with the blow then ducking to the side as it tried to attack again. She knew the bug had one weakness, she saw it when Elas dispatched the one attacking him. So, with a feline scream, Rehema leapt in as the bug missed biting her and with a groaning heave pushed it down the pile watching it roll down and land on its back where it stopped. The beetle's legs began to run in place as it fought to right itself but Rehema could care less, the thing was not a concern right now. She turned back to the center of the chamber, back to the Thaxmosis, and saw the most confusing thing the Cat had come across in a while, well at least since the library.

There, on their feet now, were the two Dragons from before and it looked like they were fighting over, of all things, an old lantern. It was the same one which was tossed across the chamber when the Ancient Dragon attacked. Really, tussling over a lantern while a beast like that Black Dragon stood a small distance away? The Serval growled again racing toward the pair wondering, no, fairly sure they were all going to die badly. As she reached the Dragons she could hear the Green one admonishing the other.

After being let go from Thaxmosis and his grip Jura had crawled quickly to Voarothim's side noting the Dragon was breathing still, only very shallow. She sighed with relief when he coughed and then helped to pull him to his feet a moment later. We have to go Jura told him. We have to get the lantern and we have to flee! The Green Dragon guided her friend over to the lantern where it lay by another large pile of coins and gems and picked up the metal vessel as Voarothim watched the fight in the chamber continue. The guards and followers of Thaxmosis were winning now, the thieves losing quickly due to the number of Monsters and Odi in the chamber. And now with Thaxmosis here adding his immeasurable strength and powers, there was no favorable end he could see for any of them, none except one.

"I have it," Jura called out standing back up.

"Open it, open it now!" Voarothim ordered turning to her and reaching for the lantern.

"Wait," Jura exclaimed refusing to let go of the vessel, "we have to flee or Thaxmosis will-"

"There is no time, we need Palaxnym!" Voarothim countered pulling at the lantern.

Then suddenly, breaking up the stalemate, Rehema appeared and took the vessel from both while gasping. "What are you two doing?"

"We need to open the lantern and free- "The Red Dragon began as Jura broke in.

"We need to flee out the secret tunnel!"

The Serval looked from one to the other, then making a decision that she was never sure why she did Rehema began to open the small door on the lantern. It should have popped open with ease but due to all the jarring and tossing the vessel had absorbed the latch was refusing to budge. Jura huffed at having to stay now and reached in trying to help the Serval open the lantern, only her fingers did more tangling with Rehema's then freeing the stuck latch. Voarothim looked away and toward Thaxmosis noting the Great Black Dragon was looking at the trio now, one of the thieves dead at his feet in a growing pool of blood.

"Hurry up, open the lantern or we are all dead."

Jura looked up and froze as her eyes locked with Thaxmosis and his voice tore into her soul like a cold knife. "What are three doing, trying to free Palaxnym maybe?"

With trembling fingers Rehema struggled to get the latch to open on the door. The shadow of the Ancient Dragon fell full on her now and the Serval fought her own body to drop the vessel and run. What was she doing trying to open this silly lantern she asked herself with scattered thoughts? The fear told her to run, the panic screamed for her to just drop the lantern and escape. Only she could not so Rehema and Jura both fought with the latch as Voarothim yelled at an approaching Thaxmosis. "We will free Palaxnym and your end will come Terrible One!"

"Oh," the Great Black Dragon grinned with evil, "I think not

Wyrmling."

Thaxmosis took a step forward, a slow step. He wanted the three to see him coming for them. He wanted the trio to see their deaths unfold slowly with no chance to stop or delay the inevitable. What happened next though Thaxmosis did not predict, could not have. He heard the Cat exclaim she had it then before she or Jura could react Voarothim snatched the lantern from her. The Red Dragon began to throw the vessel just as Thaxmosis, purely out of a reactionary impulse, roared with all his power. The sound was like an explosion, a blast of noise and air that struck the Dragons and Cat like a gale wind. The cavern shook from the tremendous shout, the roof and walls quaking. The monstrous gust of wind sent Rehema reeling and if not for Jura grabbing her and holding tight to her the Serval would have been thrown backwards into the wall behind them. Voarothim barely had time to propel the lantern back to its owner before he was fighting to stay upright from the roar of the Great Black Dragon, the robes covering him whipping and ripping from the force of the roar. He never noticed the vessel fly, buffeted by the bellow of Thaxmosis, past the Terrible One's shoulder to land behind him with an inaudible bang...the door popping open just as the roar stopped.

"There is no where you can hide, no where you can run

Voarothim to escape me!" Thaxmosis screamed after taking a breath not sure if the three could hear him after being struck by his mighty roar.

He took another step forward, toward his enemies ready to rip them all to small, insignificant pieces, when a second roar shook the cavern. The Great Black Dragon spun turning completely around to look behind him.

"THAXMOSIS!"

"No," The Great Black Dragon of Thathu hissed just before a cone of fire as tall, and just as wide as he stood enveloped him from the being exiting the lantern.

Thirteen

———— • ————

Much like Thaxmosis, Palaxnym, Dawns Herald, still remembered the days when Dragons ruled the Lands. He could recount with grand detail the flights his wide wings made as he crossed over the white caps of the tall peaks of the Argentum Mountains, part of the range which splits the Lands dividing East and West and is home to the Ursi and the Burrowers. He could remember flying over the other mountain range, the vast and wind swept craggy slopes of the Blood Peaks. So named because with the sun rise and set the metals in the mountains stone glowed blood red giving the range an eerie visage. Beyond the peaks, where he had flown several times, was nothing but the Endless Waste, a harsh land of ice and frozen tundra. Only the strong survived the Waste, those whose stubborn refusal to die or leave keeping them alive in such desolation, which is why it was the perfect land for the Giants. And like his fellow Wyrm, Palaxnym kept his dealing with the 'Tall' ones of the north to a minimum, only when desperately in need did Dawn's Herald converse with Giants. He flew high in the noon sky with the sun shining off his golden scales and skin, gleaming like a second ball of fire, and all the while with no worry except that of a challenge from another Dragon.

He remembered little of his first years out of the egg, but Palaxnym could never forget the night when the Dragons took to hiding. They had caused this...effrontery, to themselves did the Dragons. It was the war between all Wyrms for Dominance that had taken so many of their numbers. Dragon killing Dragon for nothing more than territory which was plentiful, and what did it win them in the end this war? There were not enough of the 'Immortalis Lacerta' left to fight when the new ones who inhabited the Lands now looked to end the reign of the Drake. The Dragon would have been no more, a tale told to children at bedtime if not for a fateful decision made by a gathering of the oldest of their kind, the Ageless Wyrms. The loss of their mighty wings and beautiful bodies, to be forever trapped in this human shape so as to pass through the Lands hidden was chosen over fighting till none of their kind remained. Oh yes, they would have been hunted and killed by the very ones they imitate now to live side-by-side with, but it was a necessary choice. There were some who refused to change shape and those few were murdered by Anthros, slaughtered by Humans when trapped and unable to seek escape.

Palaxnym had chosen, just like Thaxmosis and his love Ith, to be 'human' in shape and to pass through the Lands unnoticed. Giving up their natural state was hard enough, to assume another identity and life which contradicted your true sense of who you were, it was hellish but then the Dragons learned of a further consequence of living in secret. There would be no young if Wyrms lived imitating Anthros or Humans. By choosing to live without wings the mating ritual of the Sky Dance was lost to them, the ecstasy of bonding with your mate while high among the clouds gone, and without the dance there would be no eggs with young wyrmlings. That was till Palaxnym learned one day there were defectors to the decree of the Elders to hide. Years after changing his shape Palaxnym began to hear of sightings of Drakes, glimpses of the magical beasts out over the Plains of the West and other stories by Anthros and Humans telling how they witnessed of the flight of Dragons in the South. Yet, strangely, there was no physical evidence the Immortalis Lacerta had returned to the Lands and that helped in making the sightings less...convincing. The sightings were infrequent, scattered across the Lands, and always so far away from eyes which could confirm the return of Dragons that soon the sightings became yarns, stories passed around the places where people drank. The Dragons were still hidden and all was safe.

He understood why some would break the choice to hide,

to fly and dance with the one you were bonded too, but it was not till Ith came to him that he also chose to break the rule and fly once again. To be with her high in the sky Palaxnym would chance a rare sighting and then deal with what it might bring. Then the day came when he found a small Red Wyrmling on the Plains of the West, days out from the nearest of the Equine city and Palaxnym realized there was an unforeseen result of the Dragons dancing again. When the Wyrms were plentiful a wyrmling was precious but now, with so few Drakes left and the Sky Dance a rare occurrence, the offspring's were priceless and one such as Voarothim, a Red Dragon, would be double.

It is why the Gold Dragon knew Thaxmosis would hold the young Dragon as a captive.

It is why when the magical portal opened he was more than prepared to fight.

Palaxnym was ready to kill to save his wyrmling.

The Great Black Dragon threw his hands and arms up in front of his face just as the fire hit him full on. He was blinded instantly from the flare of the flames and his robes burnt away with the flash of heat leaving the Dragon covered only in his scales. The temperature was so intense the ground bubbled and hissed as the dirt burnt around Thaxmosis, the water in the air around him so superheated steam formed fogging the chamber. And still the Terrible One stood, his feet dug into the burning ground around him, refusing to falter or give in to the attack of Palaxnym. Behind him, unseen by the Dragon, Rehema gasped as she was pulled by Jura and pushed by Voarothim just before the fire was on them. She felt her fur singe while the Green Dragon screamed holding up her free hand trying to block the heat. Rehema knew if it was not for The Red Dragon behind them, if not for Voarothim using his body to shield them both, she and Jura might not have lived.

Still, behind them, Baldric could only watch in shock as the flames rolled in like a wave to take him. He had started in to kill Rehema, finish her off with his poisoned blade via a deadly backstab, only he froze when the Ancient Dragon roared. The thief/assassin was knocked backwards from the gale wind and without someone to catch him, like Rehema had, he crashed up against the wall in a lump. Baldric gained his feet and spun ready to either attack or run as fast as he could. It was just in time to see the wall of fire, just in time to know he would never be a member of the Red Remnant. Thankfully he felt little pain as the flames burned him to ash in an instant, Baldric was nothing more than a pile of glowing embers on the chamber floor. And still the flames rolled along, up the wall and then across the ceiling, burning and destroying all it touched, except for Thaxmosis. Then the flames stopped mercifully, the chamber now as hot as the swamp it sat under on a Summer day.

The Terrible One dropped his hands, which glowed from the conflagration of flames, and squinted trying to find the one who had attacked him, the one he knew was awake now. He never saw the strike as it flew over the top of his lowering hands and slammed into his jaw with enough force to make him take a step back. Thaxmosis felt his head snap to his right with a vicious pop just before a set of claws slashed across his exposed chest, long knives trying to cut past his scales to the protected flesh there, only the attempted rend failed to pierce the hide of the Great Black Dragon. As Thaxmosis turned back to see the gold tinted skin and scales of Palaxnym he saw a third strike from his nemesis coming as well as Ith climbing free of the magical lantern now. Another right fist slammed into his face and this time the force of the strike knocked Thaxmosis back two long steps as he heard Palaxnym scream.

"YOU DARE TRY TO IMPRISON MY FAMILY?"

He was reeling from his rage fueled enemy's attack. Thaxmosis was helpless to stop the next two blows that rained down on him. And amazingly he could hear the screaming of his followers as Ith exacted her own price for being locked away.

It was a circle, a large black flat circle that floated in the very air just above the ground. Rehema stood next to Jura letting the Green Dragon hold her up. Her skin was hot under her fur and she breathed deep filling her lungs with the smoky air while watching wide eyes the magical portal which projected from the lantern she was just trying to open. She had missed the tall Gold Dragon as he exited the magical space but now she stared in disbelief as yet another Dragon exited the limitless space of the circle. The Dragon was rich Blue in color and a female and very upset. Just as one of her long blue legs touched the ground she screamed, a loud screeching blast which, not as powerful as Thaxmosis, was still able to hurt the Serval's ears. As Rehema reached up and covered her ears the air around the Dragon began to crackle and hiss while the smell of ozone began to build, like right after a thunderstorm. Then, with a loud crash, a line of lightning shot across the chamber striking one Troll and exploding the monster on the spot.

"Oh please tell me she is with you?" Rehema whispered as she watched in horror.

"It is Ith, the one who raised me." Voarothim whispered, grimacing as his throat and neck ached.

"Where are the others who came with you? We must flee

now that we have the chance." Jura stated looking down to the Cat, who only looked up at her with a lost expression. Where were Elas and Lalya?

They fell, rolled, and basically tumbled down the pile of coins and jewelry trying to get away from the large scorpion, which followed right with them never letting the pair get too far from its deadly pinchers. Lalya held onto Elas with one hand keeping him close while she tried to point her sword at the bug with the other and it was damn hard to do either. Her feet found solid purchase hard to acquire and with Elas's heavy body pulling at her there was nothing Lalya could do but go with the direction they were heading. The Fox looked over her shoulder to see the floor of the chamber fast approaching then back forward to see the scorpion was approaching faster. Lalya knew the bug would attack and strike at them from above as soon as they touched the floor so she swung her sword weakly at the scorpion trying to make it slow just a step…or two or three hopefully.

The strike was so weak though due to being in such an off balanced position that the scorpion just let the blade bounce of its hard hide. We are going to be eaten like a piece of meat she thought, just as soon as the bug rips us to pieces with its claws.

Then the floor made its presence known as she and Elas hit it awkwardly, spinning even more from the landing. Her handhold on the Canine gave instantly and Lalya lost Elas, sliding away from him. The scorpion never slowed or hesitated as it went for the injured Canine, an easy kill, that was till the fireball went off flooding the chamber with heat and flame. Lalya was never sure if this sudden conflagration was magical in nature or just a trap being sprung by some unlucky fool. All she knew was in a blink there was fire all along the walls behind her and the ceiling above her, wave after burning wave. The Fox tried to scramble away from the fire as she felt her fur singe but there was nowhere to hide. She looked over to see Elas on his side covering his face, trying to block the fire while the scorpion skittered back around the pile they had just slid down seeking its own safety.

Lalya got to her feet and while bent at the waist to keep low she shuffled over to her friend. Somewhere behind a voice yelled out about imprisoning his family and she wondered who that was? Could this treasure chamber hold anymore enemy or thief? We have to be close to being at full capacity in here the Fox thought just as another loud explosion hit. Whatever it is happening behind us please let it be in our favor Lalya prayed as she reached Elas, about four steps ahead of the bug which had started back toward the pair.

"Get your sword up Elas, the bug is coming back!"

The Canine started to rise getting to one knee and holding up his sword out shakily with one arm. The other was wrapped around his torso as if holding his insides in place which meant he would not be close to full strength Lalya noted. She took a position in front of him, just to his side, putting herself between her friend and the scorpion.

"Go away bug, there will be no Anthro for you to feed on this day!" Lalya growled as Elas gained his feet finally standing tall next to her.

Behind them the din of the battle changed, more screaming and what might be pleading, the desperate sounds of the fight changing for the worse Lalya assumed. Someone screamed, another yelled back, and all the while the scorpion skittered toward the pair. It did not come straight on but took a circular strategy, its instinct telling the scorpion a full frontal charge would only get it hurt. Instead it maneuvered with ease around its prey as both claws clicked and the scorpion's stinger stabbed at the air. Lalya could hear the fight grow louder on the other side of the pile but she dared not look, to take her eyes off this bug would be a bad thing she knew. The scorpion continued to circle, its legs and feet moving in a perfectly timed dance keeping its large claws between it and the thieves, as it looked for the right moment to attack its prey.

"Here it comes, run if you can and I will hold it off." Lalya whispered sensing the bug was through waiting, its movement had slowed, the circle closing on them as it crept.

And just as she assumed her friend would not run and leave her alone, "I think I will stay and see this fight to its end."

The Fox only smiled knowing Elas, even injured, would rather stay and kill the scorpion then flee leaving his companions behind. The Canine was adorably stubborn that way. She gripped the pommel of her sword tightly with one hand as the other hand holding her dagger was loose and easy. When the bug attacked she would slash with her sword driving the claw to her left out of the way so she could deliver a stab to the back of its large head, just behind all those damn eyes. The scorpion chittered as its tail swayed slightly, its claws opened and closed with a click, and then the attack all three had waited for happened, only not as they had assumed it would. Lalya and Elas jumped and gasped as a long spear slammed into the back of the scorpion, right in the middle of its long scaled body. The point pierced the bug easily, passed through it and into the ground with such force the shaft of the weapon hummed as it shook. A shrill scream of pain came from the scorpion as it suddenly found its body pinned to the spot unable to go back or forward. The Fox blinked in shock from the abrupt appearance of the spear before looking up just as a shadow jumped from the top of the pile down into the fight in the chamber.

"I think that was the one who followed us in here." She stated in disbelief a moment before Elas screamed.

"Stop looking up there and help me kill this damn bug, please!"

The Fox gave a start at the command then jumped full into stabbing the stuck scorpion to death. Even with it stuck the bug was able to defend itself for a moment or two, but Elas and Lalya soon impaled it clean through the head and ended its life. She looked to her friend with a smile, but then someone in the other fight screamed just a blink before the whole chamber shook again, this time with a deafening thunder clap.

From her earliest memories Jura had heard stories of the Dragons of olden days and the battles which would happen high in the skies, tales told by the Terrible One. Columns of fire burning the clouds and shafts of lightning racing across the sky as Wyrms fought for supremacy of their kind. Thaxmosis would tell her how awe inspiring it was to behold the sight of two Ancient

Dragons fighting but Jura only thought it must have been awful. To see two majestic creatures such as Dragons biting at each other, claws tearing into scales and rending flesh, would have been so frightening. And now, just steps away, Jura was witnessing such a battle. She gasped as the Gold Dragon Palaxnym beat Thaxmosis with blow after blow, fist and claw trying to do nothing less than kill and destroy the Black Dragon.

And there were more Ogres and Trolls and Odi which ran into the chamber, my oh my.

Rehema reached for her sword and realized with dismay it was gone, dropped from her hand when the two Dragons saved her from the plume of fire just moments before. She began to look around for the weapon in a calm but frightened scan of the floor. Voarothim and Jura gasped and then ran from her side, presumably to help either the Blue or the Gold Dragon but which Rehema did not see. She was too busy looking for her sword, and then she spotted the pommel just a few steps away. The Serval broke and ran for it just as a Troll spotted her and started to pursue. It was a foot race, a dash for survival as Rehema ran to fetch her sword while the monster ran to kill her. Just as both reached the same point the Troll swung its clawed hand meaning to cut the Cat in half only the thief dropped into a tuck and rolled under the large appendage. With a deft move the Serval rolled up with her dagger in her left hand and her sword now in her right. She made two quick stabs with her knife to the monster's leg and then side, racing up the Troll's body as she stood up from the ground. As the monster howled and turned to her Rehema slashed with her sword across its belly spinning in a tight circle before stabbing it a third time with her dagger in its chest. All the blows knocked the monster to its knee and when it did the Serval finished it with a hard downward cut removing the Troll's head with a single lop.

The Serval took a moment to look around searching for her companions before calling out when she did not see them, "Lalya...Elas...where are you?"

There was no answer from her friends, only the sounds of the battle between the Dragons along with the approach of more guards. Oh how this had gotten so out of hand she thought turning back to the Dragons and instantly Rehema felt her heart sink.

His blows were powerful, his fists hard like stone. His claws were long and cut deep with each slash Palaxnym hit Thaxmosis with. And with each successful strike the Gold Dragon drove his nemesis farther back across the chamber, back but never down. The Great Black Dragon of Thathu refused to fall or quit so Palaxnym used his anger to fuel each attack even more. He used all his might to deliver the end blow to Thaxmosis and still the Black Dragon refused to submit. Then, with his strength used till there was no more and the anger fueling his attacks gone, Palaxnym felt his arms weaken and his fists hit with no power. Maybe the sleep potion had drained him of his boundless might and power? Maybe he was not ready to challenge such a force as Thaxmosis so soon after waking up? Whatever had caused the depletion of Palaxnym and his might, the tide of the battle changed quickly. With a single missed slash of his claws the Gold Dragon gave up the advantage and to an enemy who meant to kill him now.

With each strike his resolve grew stronger. With each blow Thaxmosis felt the power of Palaxnym lessen and his grow and when the chance came he stepped away from a slash that was pathetically weak. The Black Dragon felt the claws of his enemy barely brush his abdomen, barely scratch his scales, before launching into a devastating counter attack. He lashed out with his fists and claws just as Palaxnym had done driving into the Gold Dragon with one powerful blow after another. He drove his nemesis backwards as he had been knocked backwards, but unlike him the Gold Dragon was weaker now. The sleep potion must have depleted you Palaxnym Thaxmosis thought as slammed his fist into the stomach of his rival hard enough to lift him free of the ground. Then, as Palaxnym hung in the air for a mere moment, the Black Dragon slashed him hard with his claws driving the Gold Dragon to the ground, to one knee. Just as the Gold Dragon fell from the numerous ferocious blows and he watched as his enemy was laid low the others came for him.

"PALAXNYM!" Voarothim yelled in fear.

"NO!" Ith screamed as she watched her love succumb to the power of Thaxmosis and she reacted instantly. She let her lightning free again as she bellowed her mighty roar, the arc of energy crossing the chamber to Thaxmosis in a blinding flash.

The Great Black Dragon saw the attack coming, knew it would be Ith's response to seeing her mate collapse, and yet he only grinned as the air around him crackled and came alive with the energy of her roar. Ith was no young Dragon like Jura or Voarothim and yet she was not near as old as he or Palaxnym. She was strong this Azure Wyrm, but she was no match to the power of Thaxmosis and it was evident as he stood and let her lightning fade without so much as tickling him. When the energy died and there was nothing but the smell of ozone on the air he began to laugh.

"What was your intent Ith, to annoy me perhaps?"

"Leave Palaxnym be, come and face me!" Voarothim suddenly yelled stepping between Ith and Thaxmosis. "You do not scare me Terrible One! You never will!"

"Run Voarothim, run and get away!" Palaxnym growled stumbling to his feet. He shifted his stance and took a spot between Thaxmosis and his family. The move only made the Great Black Dragon chuckle cruelly.

"I will kill your family Palaxnym and I will make you watch me as I do it. You will see each of your loved ones die and you will live out your life seeing it over and over because I will keep you alive, fool. I will ensure your pain will be excruciating and it will be forever!"

Palaxnym gasped and fought the desire to just run at Thaxmosis striking the Dragon down again. As much as he wanted to feel the Black Dragon's blood on his claws Palaxnym knew in his weakened state he was no match for Thaxmosis and he could not endanger Ith or Voarothim any longer. There was only thing he could do and that was give his family the time need to flee this lair. He had to hold the Black Dragon at bay at the ultimate cost, to give his life so his loved ones could escape. As he watched more of Thaxmosis guards run into the chamber Palaxnym was readying his last choice, but then a young Dragon spoke up from the side bringing a small cessation to the stand-off.

"I will stay with you Thaxmosis, be whatever you wish of me, just let them go."

All eyes turned to Jura, even as Trolls and Ogres surrounded them Ith and Voarothim and Palaxnym all looked to the young Dragon as did Thaxmosis. The Black Dragon, still smiling nefariously, only shook his head. "What you offer Jura I no longer want. You betrayed me, betrayed my trust Jura, and now it looks as if you will do the same with the confidence Voarothim gave you."

The words, cold as ice, pierced Jura's heart as she forced in each breath. She turned to the Red Dragon shaking her head wanting to say no, she would never betray him or his family, and to her surprise he only shook his head with her before turning to glare at the Terrible One. "No Jura, do not believe a word his black heart says. He speaks in lies and deceit. The truth has never been a friend to Thaxmosis."

She felt her heart beat faster at his words amazingly, this close to death and the Red Dragon was still being defiant. Jura stepped over to Voarothim's side as Ith pushed both behind her intent to protect the young ones. Thaxmosis shifted his gaze from the young Dragons back to Palaxnym and growled. "I am through playing with you Palaxnym, your family dies now."

The Gold Dragon puffed out his chest, filling it with air and readying his fiery breath one last time. If he timed it right, he could hit Thaxmosis and some of the guards giving his family a chance to run for the entrance to the chamber. Yet, just as both sides were about to move, an object came flying in with such speed and force no one saw it except at the very last moment. Palaxnym thought it looked like a hammer, a large rectangle head on a shaft. The weapon flew in and struck the Black Dragon on his arm and side with a loud crunch, which was followed by an explosion of some invisible force. The blast was a thunderclap, a boom so loud and forceful it shook all three treasure chambers like an earthquake. The force was a wave bowling down everyone from the center out, the Dragons all stumbled back while the Trolls and Ogres fell to the ground in heaps. The piles of gold and gems all moved as if struck, coins and bars of silver and gold tumbling as if being thrown. Palaxnym gasped and covered his face from the thunderclap then as suddenly it happened the wave and the blast were gone. He looked up to see only his kind still standing, all but one.

Thaxmosis was so engrossed in killing the loved ones of Palaxnym and having the Gold Dragon witness it that he never glimpsed the hammer till it hit him. The head crashed into this arm and side with such force he was off his feet in an instant and flying into his guards and followers, a very large battering ram which took out a significant number of monsters. Laying there, in a tangle of Trolls and Ogres, the Great Black Dragon looked over to see the hammer he had been cradling earlier like a loving mother laying shaft up on the ground. The head was bigger now, somehow, but it was the same weapon. He tried to move his arm and growled in pain, it was broken, maybe shattered.

Then someone yelled to him, a voice he had grown to hate with all his being because he was fairly sure now it was filled with mocking contempt for him.

"I TOLD YOU, OH TERRIBLE ONE, WE ARE NOT DONE TALKING YET!"

Fourteen

After hitting with a jolting landing, after rolling and sliding down the large pile of gold coins and other treasure to the ground, Jared laid still for a moment gathering his senses and catching his breath. His back and shoulder hurt, his lungs burned, and he was not very sure of where he ended up in the chamber. Jarred had barely moved the Dragon when he hit it, and he was moving with all the strength he could manage from running. Then Thaxmosis just tossed him like a rag doll, all the way...to somewhere. He rolled over and got to his feet shakily just as his ears picked up the sounds of battle, not so faint and not too distant. He had to get back to them, his...friends? Could he call them friends, these thieves and Dragons, when he knew next to nothing of them? They had barely exchanged names, and yet strangely the Paracletus found he could not leave them to whatever fate the Black Dragon had waiting for them. Then Jared realized, with a strange calm, he was not going back to save those he had just met. No, there was no 'protecting the weaker' in this action. This was pure revenge, a deep dark desire to hurt

Thaxmosis. He wanted to maim the Dragon, leave him bloodied and broken and this feeling left him even more confused than the other reason to go back.

"I do not understand either way, only that these swords I brought will never harm that thick hide of Thaxmosis." Jared whispered still looking around. He was still trying to understand what he was feeling. This need to go back to face the Black Dragon, was it for revenge or to help the others?

As he searched the part of the treasure chamber, his eyes came across a broken pedestal on which a strange looking hammer sat. Jared stood staring at the weapon, it was nothing like he had ever seen, what with the small head on the shaft. How was that supposed to hurt someone in armor much less the scales of an Ancient Dragon? He had seen picks, deadly spiked clubs, and even morning stars and maces, but what was this compared to those menacing tools of death? Still, Jared could not look away and before he could stop what he was doing he crossed the opening and picked up the hammer. Instantly a sharp tingle went up his arm, the muscles in his arm twitching for a moment, and the shaft of the weapon began to glow a little brighter. The archaic words on the metal shaft glowed too as did some on the side on the small head of the hammer which abruptly appeared. Then he watched breathlessly as the head began to grow, expand

and stretch to the point where it looked like any normal hammer, not oversized or anything like that.

It was just normal now...but so not normal.

"What is this?" Jared hissed holding the weapon up and staring at it more. It was light, not what you would expect a hammer of this size to weigh.

As he stood there dumbfounded by what he was holding he heard a muffled sound, like someone trying to speak through a wall. The Paracletus turned around looking for the one who was speaking but there was no one else near, not a soul. Then he concentrated a little more and his ears picked up where the voice was coming from, just down by his feet. There, leaning up against the pedestal, were two simple swords.

"Just as plain as you my friend?" Jared asked looking back to the hammer. He said the words expecting nothing but silence in return, and yet he was given one. A shimmer rolled across the head of the hammer, a shine which made the weapon almost life like. "What are you?"

The was no answer this time, no shine or shimmer. Jared sighed then reached down and took both of the swords and slung the pair across his back, the pommels sitting just behind the right shoulder. The hammer had a small ring on the end of its shaft and he used it to hook the weapon to his belt before drawing one the swords, the shorter of the two. It looked like one of the swords the Simians carried only this one was shorter and glowed like the hammer, a faint shine that seemed to come from the inside. It was light as well, easily wielded with one hand, so Jared drew the second and was amazed even more. It was the perfect match to the first, not in looks, but in heft and it was sharpened on both sides.

"Now I can face you Thaxmosis, now I can meet you fairly." Jared whispered sheathing both of his blades. Yes, these swords were his now he decided and the muffled voice? Well, it was louder now and it seemed to be singing.

Jared turned his attention finally to following the sounds of the battle, which was easier because the din was louder as well. He ran toward noise but not an all-out pace, no, he took each step with care making sure of his footing. Falling down the pit earlier was a lesson well learned for the young Paracletus. The last problem Jared needed now was to drop down some chute to another pit. Still, he did not trot back to the fight and along the way he saw another rack of weapons and a very nice looking spear resting on the rotting wood structure. With a wide swing he sprinted past and grabbed the spear in his left hand and then he was back running toward the battle and in a moment he was there. Jared climbed one of the countless piles of coins with three jumps reaching the top and when he looked down on what had become of the battle he was shocked.

"There are more Dragons?" He whispered in disbelief because now, amazingly, there was a Gold Dragon and a Blue one. The Gold one had been thrashed by Thaxmosis solidly, and now he was trying to stand, gather himself while the Blue one was standing like a protective mother in front of the other two, the Green and Red Dragon from before.

A scream caught his attention and he turned his head to see the Fox and the Canine trying to keep a nasty looking scorpion from eating them. When did a large scorpion join the fight, and whose side is it on? There was no time to try and find an answer for either question he knew as Jared shifted and faced the pair at the bottom of the pile. He pulled his left arm back and with all his power he threw the spear at the scorpion hitting it in its long body, dead center almost, and pinning it to the spot. As the Fox looked up Jared spun back to the Dragons just in time to see the Gold One ready to attack, but it would garner him nothing more than a quick death Jared knew. The Gold Dragon was weak and was no match for the might of Thaxmosis, but he was with his new weapons. Jared unhooked the hammer from his belt as he ran toward the Terrible One and drew it back with his right arm, straining all his muscles to put as much power into the attack as he could. Then with a heave he threw the hammer at Thaxmosis while screaming out with all the air in his lungs.

"MORNAUG CALAUN!"

Where did these words come from? Jared had never uttered such words in his long life and yet both just rolled off his tongue in a warlike scream as the hammer flew toward Thaxmosis like an arrow shot from a bow. He watched as Thaxmosis never even moved to block the weapon. Even with his loud scream the Black Dragon just stood there till the weapon hit him with full force, which is when the true magic of the hammer was revealed. Jared could have never dreamt of this kind of power; to him a hammer was nothing more than something to drive in a peg or knock out a dent in hot metal. It could be used to lay a man or Anthro low with a hard blow, but to explode with the force of a thunderclap, well that was something he never knew could exist.

The chamber shook from the force that was released, the energy spreading out from the center which was Thaxmosis. A wave of force so powerful and strong it swept away from the middle of the chamber knocking Troll and Ogre down while tossing Anthro and Human aside like they were nothing. Large cracks formed and ran along the ceiling from the effect of the hammer blow but Jared was only looking to Thaxmosis and it was his turn to smile with just a touch of malice at the sight of the Black Dragon being thrown into his guards and ending up on his backside.

"I TOLD YOU, OH TERRIBLE ONE, WE ARE NOT DONE TALKING YET!" Jared could not help but scream out to the Dragon from atop another pile of gold. His voice was filed with contempt and with another yell he ran down the pile of treasure drawing both swords.

Voarothim watched with jaw agape as the Paracletus ran with full speed right into the guards around Thaxmosis. The whole chamber still hummed with the effect of the hammer's blast and now it was filing with screams of the Ogres and Trolls who found themselves beset upon by the devil known as Jared Sinn.

"Who is that?" Ith asked grabbing his arm as he helped steady her.

"It is Jared Sinn. He is a Paracletus!" Voarothim laughed.

"He is a What?" Ith snapped as she pulled the young Dragon over to Palaxnym, who had begun turning to his family. "How do you know that?"

"We talked with him in the library Thaxmosis keeps." Voarothim answered as Palaxnym grabbed his other arm. A chunk of the ceiling fell into the chamber, not enough to cause a collapse but just the right amount to cause concern for being crushed.

"Are you hurt?" Palaxnym yelled. All the guards of the Great Black Dragon were now in full retreat from the falling ceiling and Jared Sinn.

The Red Dragon shook his head and smiled amazingly, "I am fine but Jura knows a way out of here and I think we should take it."

"Who?" Ith and Palaxnym both asked at the same time.

Voarothim only led them both back to Jura, who watched with some satisfaction as the Black Dragon's guards dragged him from his precious treasure chamber, fleeing in the worst way from the swords of the young Paracletus. She could not take her eyes away from watching the being she hated so much being defeated, so much so she only turned away when a familiar hand touched her arm and she turned to see his handsome eyes.

"Which way is the secret tunnel Jura?"

She shook her head clearing it of the joy she was reveling in and spoke quickly. "It is over this way, behind a rock." Jura took Voarothim's hand in hers and began to lead the group, but not before looking to Rehema. "Get your friends, we need to leave now!"

"Do not worry, we will follow you out." Rehema answered back before calling out to the chamber, chunks of the ceiling falling in still. "Lalya, Elas, where are you?"

From behind a pile of treasure the pair stumbled and the Fox waved to her, "over here, Elas is hurt."

All at once the group broke and ran for the back of the chamber, the Dragons moving slow enough to let the three thieves follow as the Fox and the Canine fell in with them. They ran weaving past pile after pile of gold when suddenly Jura broke from them and ducked into a small alcove near the back of the chamber.

"Jura, what are you doing?" Voarothim yelped with surprise. If the chamber did not collapse and kill them all then a certain Black Dragon might, so to linger was not the best of ideas he thought. Then she appeared again and took his hand in her while smiling.

"One last task!"

The Red Dragon just shook his head and let her lead them to a spot along the back wall well away from any gold. It was just the usual cavern wall, mostly roughhewn rock, with the exception of a very large and very out of place boulder. Jura stopped by it and turned back to the group. "There, we move the boulder and there is a tunnel behind it."

Voarothim looked to Palaxnym who shook his head and looked to Jura, "a boulder that must weigh more than we can move."

"Oh," Jura giggled and looked to Voarothim, "it is not a real boulder, just a facade. Go, you should be able to move it easily."

The Red Dragon looked again to the one he had always called father and when the Gold Dragon only nodded he turned and gave the large boulder a shove. It moved with a push, not as easily as Jura said, but it moved nonetheless and that made him smile. As Voarothim pushed the rock away to expose the tunnel Ith looked to Jura with a confused look.

"If you knew this was a way out and away from Thaxmosis why did you not take it before today?"

Jura looked to the Blue Dragon and there was a bit of shame in her expression. She spoke low as Voarothim finished moving the boulder. "I have never been outside, in that strange world. Where would I go? Who would I trust? I would have been as lost out there as I was in here with Thaxmosis."

"Well you can come with us Jura. You can trust us and we will show you where you belong." Voarothim answered and his words almost made her cry as she looked to him. Even Ith felt a tug at her heart, from what the Green Dragon had confessed and what the one she called son had said.

"Yes Jura, it is time to go." Palaxnym remarked while holding out his hand motioning her to take the first steps out of the tunnel. The Gold Dragon knew this moment was more important than anything to Jura, the choice to leave this prison had to be hers. And with a smile he watched as she did just that, not with small scared steps but long confident ones, and Jura left all that was her old life behind. The scene was not missed by the others, especially a certain pair.

Elas turned to the Fox and sighed with a grin, "are you crying?"

"No," Lalya hissed wiping her eye and grinning as well, "I got dirt in my eyes saving your furry rump. Can we just leave this pit before we die, please?"

The Serval only shook her head and followed the Dragons leaving the treasure chamber behind and the trap it had become. She wondered about Jared, was he going to get away? He had to know to kill the Dragon who ruled this lair would be impossible. There were too many guards and the Dragon may be wounded but it was not ready to die. Would he flee through this tunnel? Maybe there was another way out he could take? All Rehema was sure of was Jared had to get away because she was sure the Dragon would not take him prisoner like he had with Jura.

The first guard to fall before his blade was a Troll with a large green body. Jared felt the scimitar slice easily through the flesh and even the bone as took the monster's arm off at the elbow with a downward slash. The double edged blade in his left followed with a stab through its throat and as it fell to the ground Jared was already moving on to his next foe, an Ogre with a large axe in one of its hands. Behind the large grey monster, he could see the other guards dragging Thaxmosis toward the entrance to the chamber. They were helping their master escape, to run away, and to the young Paracletus that was quite unacceptable. As the Ogre swung the axe on a flat plane intent on cutting him in half Jared jumped up letting the blade pass beneath him, only as it passed beneath his feet he kicked down and used the surface of the axe like a spring board. All at once Jared was spinning and flying, a full circle. The sword in his left hand came round and with a vicious cut sliced through the Ogre's neck almost cleaving the large orb free from the monster's shoulders.

As the monster fell next to the injured, but regenerating, Troll the other guards started to see the reality of this new enemy, which was this foe was not some poor thief who stumbled into the wrong lair. Oh no, he was so much more, deadly. One Odi stepped up though and tried to impale Jared on a spear, much as he had done to the scorpion, only Jared brought the scimitar down and cut the shaft of the spear with ease. There was no crack of the wood pole breaking or shattering, just the hiss of a clean cut, like a hot knife through creamy butter. If there was any courage left to the guards after watching two of their ilk fall, then what little remained disappeared as the spear point fell to the ground. The Odi stared at his broken weapon then up looked up to Jared with a snap, just in time to feel the slap of the scimitar's blade as the flat struck him a blow hard enough to knock him unconscious.

"Where are you running Terrible One? Why not face me Thaxmosis? Why are running oh Great Black Dragon?" Jared yelled as he lashed out and took down another Troll followed by a second Ogre, one missing both arms and the other its right leg and hand.

"You are nothing to one like me Jared Sinn! You are no

Paracletus, no Dominum Summum! I do not fear you!"
Thaxmosis screamed back even as his guards ushered him from
the chamber. In truth the Black Dragon knew in his injured state
he was no match for either the Paracletus or the Gold Dragon and
retreat was the only choice to keep his long life. Yet it still pained
him to no end to leave that fool untouched.

"Then come and face me Dragon! Come and face me!"
Jared bellowed as he took down two more Odi, his blades cutting
them down with ease.

There would be no final fight, no final confrontation. As
Jared looked on, blood dripping from his swords and hands, the
guards for Thaxmosis ensured their master's escape. The
Paracletus watched as one of the last Odi reached into a hidden
spot in the wall and pulled something, maybe a lever? The tunnel
leading into the chamber, the only way in, toppled and caved in
with a small rumble. A cloud of dirt rolled out from where the
entrance used to be crossing the ground just at ankle level,
moving over Jared's boots. He stood staring at the rubble for a
moment before yelling.

"One day I will come back for you Thaxmosis and when I
do there will be no place where you can run away from me! No
place you may hide! Go and live your long life knowing this!"

Then, with it done and the anger spent, Jared cleaned and

sheathed both of his swords. The ceiling looked stable now, the large parts had stopped falling now he noted. He took a look around after picking up his hammer all the while thinking, be a shame not to see what else might be tucked away in the chamber, but then another thought stopped that one. You did not come here for gold or gems or the such. You came for answers which you have now, and these fine weapons, and that is enough for this day. To take any coin or jewelry would only make that seem…less noble. Yes, he told himself as he walked away leaving the dead and injured behind without a glance back, he had come for one thing and he had that now. So he went the way the others took, followed their path which was easy to trace, and Jared ended up by the back wall with the opened tunnel now. Without stopping or looking back he disappeared into the tunnel happy to be free of this place, even though he had his answers Jared did not like what he had to do to obtain those answers.

"My treasure chamber…I have lost my precious treasure chamber!" Thaxmosis yelled with rage grinding his teeth.

"Yes Master, but you are alive and we can dig the entrance out again." The Troll Shaman said and when the cold eyes of the Black Dragon turned to him his heart slowed to a crawl.

"Then start digging, all of you." Thaxmosis snarled, his voice dropping into a growl that went on for a bit. The guards were intimate with the sound. It was the one the master made before he melted you with his acid spit.

Still, even as his followers quickly went to the monumental task of digging out the tunnel, the Black Dragon seethed. He knew they were on the other side taking his gold, those thieves and that Paracletus, robbing him of all the gold he had rightfully stole from others. He could barely control his anger before turning and screaming down the tunnel. "And someone bring me new robes!"

He would not leave till this tunnel was clear and he could see his gold again. This, Thaxmosis had decided.

The sun was coming up when they reached the outside, the tunnel leading the group of Dragons and Anthros out to a section of the Thathu swamp rarely if ever visited. The opening was in the middle of a small rise, the small hill jutting up and out of the ground with nothing else nearby. Jura held up her hand as the bright light from the rising sun hurt her eyes. She felt Voarothim reach his arm under and around her arm to help steady her. Jura had only been outside once, so long ago it was a distant memory, and for the moment the smells and sounds of the world assailed her. And yet the Green Dragon would not change her new world for the old, not one moment for anything. She would never go back underground she had decided with every step away from Thaxmosis. She would be free, now and forever, though 'free' meant having the help of these new Dragons.

"It is fine Jura. I will not let you fall." Voarothim whispered.

"Thank you," she whispered back squeezing his hand.

The group moved down the slope and into the swamp a good distance, the need to get away from the tunnel opening a dire necessity. Thaxmosis could, and probably would, send someone round to try and intercept them and in their present condition that would be the end of them all. With caution the group went into the swamp covering their escape carefully before Palaxnym had them stop on a dry piece of land. He turned to the Anthros and spoke plainly with a cold assertion.

"We will be going our own way from here. Follow us at your peril."

Rehema heard the words and also the intent which came with each and every one. She looked to the four Dragons and only nodded. "We have no business in the direction you are going. Our only business was down there in the treasure chamber and unfortunately that came to a very disappointing end."

"You did not get 'The Eye of the Moon'. Your brother will be killed." Voarothim whispered as if jolted by the news.

Before the Serval could answer him though Jura smiled with her eyes practically closed to keep the painful rays of the sun out. "No, her brother will be fine. Here Voarothim, give her this."

The Red Dragon looked at her perplexed, one eyebrow raised at her statement, till she handed him a very large diamond. It was shaped into a smooth ball, polished till it was clear with no blemish or mark. No hand could create such perfection and yet here it sat in the Dragon's palm gleaming in the sun. That alone would make the gem remarkable, priceless, except in the center of this excellence was a second round sapphire, its blue color matching the azure scales of Ith. Voarothim stared at the gem for a moment feeling a sudden urge not to hand it over to the Serval, not till the calm hand of Ith touched his shoulder and she spoke to him.

"I am sure they are in need of the gem more than you are Voarothim."

"Yes, yes they are." The Red Dragon smiled and handed the gem, gently with reluctance, to the Serval.

She took it carefully before looking to Jura with a small smile. "Thank you Jura, and my brother thanks you." Rehema said hoping her relief could be heard as well as seen.

"You are welcomed Rehema, I hope to see you again one day." Jura said, her smile hiding her thoughts.

"Yes, maybe we will see each other again." The Serval replied, her smile also hiding her own thoughts. She wondered still about Jared Sinn, did he escape the treasure chamber? As the Dragons walked away leaving the thieves alone in the swamp Rehema stole a look back toward where the exit of the tunnel should be.

May I see you again one day as well Jared Sinn she thought one last before turning and heading in the opposite direction of the Dragons.

He walked out the tunnel and also found the sun rising. Jared looked around, did not see any of the group, and grinned. It was for the best to go unnoticed, to be alone right now he thought as he disappeared into the swamp. He was not entirely sure if he was the Lord of the fabled Paracletus, but he did know the Lands were not ready for their return. If the Anthros had need of their Protectors then the rulers of each race would have brought them back long before now, but there was no call and as such he could only surmise the need for the Paracletus was not great enough.

So Jared slipped into the swamp silently traversing his way through the trees and water for the better part of the morning. He finally found the entrance to the lair of Thaxmosis again but instead of entering just passed it without a look back. Later he came across the hiding spot of his possessions, not much except for what was needed to camp. Jared threw on his pack and continued on moving.

There was a certain Weasel he needed to talk with, desperately.

Epilogue

———— • ————

Four days later…

They were almost home, and yet still so far away Palaxnym thought as once more the Dragons trek came to a halt. He watched with a small smile as Voarothim talked with Jura, explaining excitedly that what had caught her attention was a nest of birds. Locked away for her whole life in the lair of Thaxmosis the Green Dragon, majestic Wyrms who once ruled the forest, Jura knew nothing of the outside world. At the edge of the Thathu swamp the Dragons had come across a field of bright yellow butterflies and the sight made Jura cry and then laugh as Voarothim took her by the hand and ran after the small flying creatures. When the Red Dragon caught one he stood perfectly still holding the butterfly in his hands so Jura could touch it gently at first, then stroke its gossamer wings, and then finally hold it herself till it took to the air once more. Such 'breaks' had happened, were still happening, several times a day as Palaxnym watched Voarothim and Jura walk off the small trail to get a closer look at the birds.

"We needed to stop anyway." Ith suddenly spoke taking his attention away from the young ones to her. His mate's smile was beautiful and warm and it made his heart beat faster

"Yes, we were tired from keeping such a frantic pace." He replied with a smile. It was good to hear her voice, his mate Ith. She had chosen to keep her distance from him after the escape from the claws of Thaxmosis, angry for the obvious reason.

His plan had gone horribly wrong, to say it mildly, and if not for the appearance of the mysterious young Paracletus his family might have perished or been imprisoned by the Black Dragon. Palaxnym had borne his punishment, her coldness and quiet, without word until last night when she asked him why he had risked the life of Voarothim, why he had risked all their lives. He produced the book the young Dragon had given him just moments after their escape and opened it to a certain page and passage. He turned it to let her read what was written, and after her eyes scanned the words she looked up to him with worried eyes whispering low.

"His mother is Balanur?"

He only nodded and slid closer, "yes, one of the worst of all the Wyrms. She has betrayed her kind, destroyed other Dragon eggs, and even killed her own wyrmlings. Between Thaxmosis cruelty and her treachery I would be hard pressed to choose which Wyrm is worse."

"But why would she want another wyrmling after what she did to her first one?" Ith asked quickly. It was a riddle which had plagued him from the moment he had assumed Voarothim was her offspring the Gold Dragon explained. He continued when she only nodded for him too. It was why he had to have the book, to confirm his suspicions, and now that he was assured of Voarothim's mother the reason such a malice filled Wyrm would want a young one tortured his mind now more than before. She has a plan, some scheme Ith replied, she has always been the schemer and deceiver. He only nodded and put the book away before speaking, and that was not the only part of this he was worried about.

You are afraid he will be like her and his kind, take up the mantle of the Fire Drake and be a destroyer Ith asked? Yes, he answered low, if he learns of his true lineage will he follow those infamous ones who had come before him? Will he take up with their ways and bring fire to this word to watch it burn? Ith only shook her head while reaching up to caress his human looking face. Oh how beautiful she was in her true form Palaxnym thought at that moment, her long neck and wide wings. You will show him another way my love, the way you showed me. We Blue Dragons, we were brutal in our own ways and yet you showed me another path and I have never been sorry for walking next to you.

Yes, he thought as he leaned into her hand, my sweet mate was right as always. One day he would have to tell Voarothim of his kind, their ways, and let the young one decide how he will live his long life.

"How far are we from Lostfall?" Ith asked bringing Palaxnym's thoughts back to the now of the day. It was the name of an old outpost high up in the Cloudbreak Mountains, one of the many mountain ranges which made up the long and awesome Spires of the Sky. The outpost had long been abandoned and forgotten by the Ursi who lived below and the few Mustelidae who lived above. It was the perfect home for the Dragons, a large enough space to allow them to live and hidden away from any and every one.

He looked up the trail then back to her, "maybe a night, that is if Jura does not find another thing which intrigues her and which Voarothim must spend an hour explaining."

The Blue Dragon laughed sitting next him, her body leaning up against him slightly as they waited patiently for their young ones to appear again. "Do you think Jared Sinn is a Paracletus, the actual young one of the last Dominum Summum?"

The Gold Dragon turned and looked to her, his smile slighted now. "I do not know truthfully, but he did move like us, as fast as us. From what I have been told, what Cenloth wrote in his book, was the Lord of the Paracletus was the only one of their kind endowed with our essence, the spirit of the Wyrm. It was done to ensure only his young would be the true Lord of the Paracletus, Guardians of the Races. So the chances are good Jared Sinn is the Lord Supreme and rightful leader of the fabled Protectors."

"No other King but the true blood heir may rule?" Ith remarked and Palaxnym only nodded before she asked the question which worried her. "If he is the true Dominum Summum then do you think he will raise the walls of Pallator again?"

It took a moment for him to answer and again it was only an assumption. "He may, but if he does then Jared Sinn must face more than just rebuilding a castle. He must find the truth of that night 80 years long past, dig it up if need be, and then accept whatever it is he finds."

"It seems he walks the same path as our Voarothim." Ith stated, the last said on purpose and caught by the vigilant ears of the Gold Dragon.

"Yes, it does seem that is the course both must take." He agreed. The pair waited patiently, talking more and feeling happy to be so close to home.

In the eastern forest, among the large oaks and pines, built on the rolling hills at the foot of the Cloudbreak mountains, sits the grand city of Thesedell. Behind two sets tall walls of stone, through busy streets in the lower districts and elegant buildings on the upper quarter, on top of the tallest hill and past a set of iron gates sits the large castle which the pride of Leos and the pack of Mastiffs call home, the rulers of the Daes. The members of both families were seen outside the walls of their abode quite frequently, neither the Lions nor the Danes were ones to stay hidden in their castle. They preferred nice spring days when the heat was not too much and with a gentle wind so they could walk the streets of their city greeting and speaking with the citizens of Thesedell.

In the lower district the crowd at The Broken Shield pub was a raucous one, and it was just past midday on a work day which meant it should have been empty. This lack of patronage was the reason Rehema chose The Broken Shield as a place to meet with her companions and brother Sefu. As she was bumped by a drunken fighter for the tenth time, he kept screaming about searching for a dungeon to raid and she was close to giving him the location of Thaxmosis and his lair, the Serval was beginning to think it was time to go. The table they all sat at was in a corner and should have been more secluded but she felt they could have talked in the middle of the street outside and had a quieter conversation. She heard a small chuckle and looked up to see the handsome face of Drax with a smile, his long, brown fur covered body leaning up against his love Elas.

"I know that look,"

"What look?" Rehema asked back quickly while smiling as well.

"He knows your thinking about telling that fighter where the Dragon's lair is." Elas chuckled before drinking from his mug of mead.

Drax pouted a little then laughed with his love, "I say tell him and let us see if he is worth his talk."

Rehema only raised an eyebrow as her smiled turned a little wicked. To her left her brother Sefu, a perfect match in looks except for his larger size and thicker tail, spoke up. "He could never match our friends here in battle, but it would be fun to see if he could."

"Yes, yes," Drax exclaimed holding up his small mug, "if not for the beautiful Rehema, the heroic Lalya, and the stout Elas you might be without your head. I hear Kazmir rarely rescinds one of his punishments, especially for working in his city without permission."

Sefu only nodded looking to his sister with a small wink, "Oh I know how lucky I am to have such a sibling. She has saved my life more than once."

The Serval only nodded as Lalya leaned in, "wait, how come Rehema is beautiful and Elas is stout but I'm just heroic?"

The Puma took a sip of wine and shook his head, "being heroic is sometimes better that being beautiful Lalya."

"And when is that?"

"When you saved my precious Elas, for now you are the greatest hero I know." Drax purred reaching under the table to rub the Canine's leg with long strokes.

The Fox chuckled shaking her head before turning to her friend, "so all is settled Reh, Kazmir is good?"

"Yes, I gave the gem to Digger as instructed and he will hand it over to whoever is next in line. We, including Sefu, are once again in the good graces of The Rat." Rehema answered as one of the serving girls bumped into her this time.

"And that is the most heroic thing I have ever heard." Sefu

chuckled just as the drunk fighter started a fight at the other end of the pub.

"And that, my friends, is the cue saying it is time to go." Lalya sighed and everyone around the table agreed.

The group paid the tab and headed for the door with Elas and Sefu making a hole in the crowd for them to pass. Once on the street they all agreed to meet again tomorrow at a less visited establishment to talk about what was to come next. Then all went their separate ways and Rehema found herself alone walking back to the small house she rented alone, it was not much but it had an open air porch she loved. As she walked Rehema stole a quick look over her shoulder every now and then making certain she was not followed in arriving home. The door was locked, the small wire at the top unbroken which meant no one had entered her abode, not by the front door at least. Rehema stepped in and quickly closed and locked the door. She checked the small flat and found no one present, all the windows shuttered and locked. Assured she was still alone Rehema undressed and slipped into a long shirt she wore when by herself and nothing else before heading for the porch to sit and watch the city lackadaisically for the rest of the afternoon. When she walked out of her bedroom though she instantly knew she was no longer alone, and it was because she could see a shadow out on the porch now.

"Come kitten, I brought us a bottle of the Regent's best wine and it would be a travesty not to drink it."

The voice was one she had grown to love over these last years, and not as a mentor but as one she would willingly spend her life with forever. Rehema sighed and walked out on the porch to see Kazmir sitting in of the two chairs, the small table which was supposed to be between the chairs moved to his right. His legs were outstretched with his feet resting on the stone wall of the porch, both of his shoes were off and his shirt was open to his abdomen she noted while sauntering up. Maybe he will stay the night? She would like that very much. The chair left for her was turned with the seat facing him, a perfect invitation Rehema thought as she started to take a seat.

"You could have told me you were coming. I would have left the front door open for you to come in."

"No need," Kazmir smiled handing her a glass of wine, "I let myself in. Really kitten, a single wire across the top hinge, not much of a challenge."

"I would never lock you out my master, especially since the house here is yours." She replied playfully with a wink.

"The house is mine? I do not remember selling it to you?"

He played along smiling.

"You gave it to me my master," she purred taking her legs and laying them across his lap and cozying up, "for services rendered, do you remember the theft of the Jasmine Dagger?"

The Rat gasped and nodded at the mention of the famous dagger as his free hand reached down and began to caress her thigh lovingly, "ah yes, that was a nasty affair. I am glad you took care of that so quickly, and quietly. Well worth the price of this abode."

Rehema smiled and sipped the wine, which was quite good, and looked out on the city from her perch. Then she turned back and stepped into the world she had been a part of for some time now, his. "What movements have the Remnant been making while I was away?"

He turned to her and even though he wanted her free and clear of this business with the Assassins Guild Kazmir could not lie to her. In truth he never could. "I do not think they thought very highly of Baldric or his skill. They brought in a fresh body while you and he were out, filling the open spot he was to take I presume."

"They were right, he was a terrible thief and an even worse assassin." Rehema remarked sipping the wine again, reveling in his touch. She wondered how Kazmir knew about the inner working of the former Assassins Guild then thought to be in the dark on this was better than being enlightened. "Do you think the Remnant will make another attempt on you again?"

"No, not soon anyways. They know now I had their man in my sights before he even knew I knew. I want to say thank you kitten, for taking care of such business."

"I would protect you with my life my master, without question." She whispered smiling. And she would because when she discovered the Remnant was paying to have him killed Rehema went to Scars and demanded to know where Kazmir was and if he was safe. The stoic, and scary, human only nodded and said The Rat was fine and he had even thought of a plan to draw out the assassins from the shadows, it involved Kazmir being bait though. Without even a blink she told Scars she would be the bait in his stead. So convincing were her words that the usual cold Scars smiled and told her he would pass on her request.

"Stop calling me that, please." He quickly said, almost snapping, but then gathered his patience and spoke calmly. "When it is just us two please call me by name. You are so much more to me than just a lowly thief, a common larcener in my fold."

His words, the closest Kazmir had ever come to speaking

his heart, struck her with a happiness that made Rehema's heart skip. There were no words to reply to him with she could think of at the moment so she only smiled warmly and nodded as his hand slid up her leg just a little more. "I would have asked anyone else to go and retrieve the gem kitten-"

"There was no one else Kazmir, no one else you knew could bring you the gem…no one else you could trust." She finished for him. It was the plan from the start she learned from Kazmir himself, to kill two birds with one arrow.

The guild was being paid quite a sum of gold to retrieve a certain gem from the lair of a very dangerous enemy, a Dragon. Once Kazmir learned of the job, it's location and the mark who they would be stealing from, he came up with a plan to rid himself of the bounty on his head. The Remnant had no clue what Kazmir looked like, only that he was either seven feet tall or five foot and mysterious. So The Rat let the word spread out in the city he was sending three thieves out to bring back a gem, a gift to get one's brother back into his good graces. All a ruse, Sefu was never in danger and Kazmir knew the Remnant would send along one of their assassins to steal the gem and then use it as a means to draw him out. Once the Unseen Hand took on a job it was fulfilled, completed, or Kazmir would see to its conclusion personally so the Remnant figured The Rat would come out of hiding to get back the gem. Too bad for poor Baldric, The Rat's honed instincts had him two steps ahead of the thief/assassin and when he begged pathetically to offer his assistance to Scars Kazmir knew who the traitor would be. Kazmir told Rehema to be careful, to let the three humans die at the hands of the Dragon. He wanted her hands clean of any blood and when she told him what happened in the lair Kazmir only smiled and nodded, thankful his plan had not killed his kitten.

The Rat only nodded and sighed, the weight on his heart eased. She watched him relax while sipping more of the incredible wine then spoke. "What happens to The Eye of the Moon now?"

"It goes to the one who paid for us to 'obtain' it for them."

"And you have no idea who that is, right?" She asked with a raised eyebrow playfully squeezing the muscles in her legs as he caressed trapping his hand.

Kazmir shook his head, "no kitten, I do not know who paid our fee but in this business that is usual. We ask no questions and make only one demand."

"Where is the gold we agreed on?"

The Rat laughed and nodded. "Half up front and half when the task is completed. Always get a down payment kitten, remember that."

It was good to hear him laugh, it was a strong hearty sound which made Rehema smile even more. She sighed warmly filled with contentment, "do you trust Digger with the task of handing the gem over and getting the Guild's gold?"

He looked to her and winked, "I have another set of eyes watching him as we speak. When it comes to a payday I always double down kitten."

"Is it Scars?"

"No," He answered shaking his head before sipping some wine, "he's looking into other business, personal. I have Three Fingers following him."

Rehema giggled suddenly at the mention of the thief, "do you think it is wise to have Digger followed by a human who lost two fingers because he was caught stealing?"

"Do you know how Digger got his name? He robs graves at night, digs the damn boxes right up out of the freshly turned dirt. And he is not that smartest when doing it, fool dug up the wrong graves and caught something. I think two nitwits doing a delivery job will be safe. They will cancel each other out."

She gasped at the information then broke out laughing.

Oh how she loved her master she thought as the afternoon went on and Rehema enjoyed every second she spent with The Rat. And when evening came and it was time to turn in her silent prayer to have him stay was pleasantly answered with his presence in her bed.

Out on the dark streets of Thesedell a cloaked form moved though the people with ease, barely drawing any attention. He was hooded and drawn inward giving little for anyone to see of his appearance. Down along the main streets he passed without a glance in his direction and when he disappeared into the shadows of an alley he was truly invisible. So was the life of Digger the Grave Robber. Digger had learned through many a year of doing his profession that secrecy was the best friend he could have. The less people who know what you do and who you are the better life a grave robber lives, judgmental people were everywhere it seemed. He reached up and scratched at the strange rash on his portly face and decided he had to see the apothecary again tomorrow. The salve he had prepared for him, this batch was the sixth, was not working at all to relieve the damnable itching. Maybe this time he would tell apothecary how he got the rash, digging up the wrong grave? Really, the people who put up the headstones up should say how the person died, if it was from a strange disease or what not. It certainly would keep the chance of catching something undiagnosable to a minimal risk.

Digger took a turn and went down another dark alley blending in with the dark, keeping in the shadows till he reached a door at the end of the passage. He knocked twice, waited, and knocked twice again. There was a simple knock back, like a staff striking the wooden floor, and Digger knew it was the place. He entered the room, it was barely lit by a single candle, and noticed it was bare of any furniture or belonging except for a small table in its center. There was a single individual standing on the other side of the table, at least seven feet tall dressed in a black cloak which covered robes of the same color and a cowl pulled down so the face was hidden from prying eyes. Digger closed the door behind him slowly, with some trepidation as he felt a little fear being in the room alone with the being.

"I am here with what you asked us to retrieve. It is yours with Kazmir's appreciation. He thanks you for your business and wishes you a long life. By the way, where is the gold you agreed to upon delivery, if I may be so forward to ask?"

The being did not speak, not a sound or word, only pointed with a hand covered in a long glove to the table and there suddenly sitting in the middle was a very large sack of gold. Digger was sure it was not there before, or at least he was somewhat sure. It was so dark in the room he could have walked through and missed a wall in the back. He walked over and opened the drawstring making sure it was gold coins in the sack with one eye while the other kept a close eye on the strange cloaked person. When Digger was satisfied with what was inside the sack he reached into his cloak, very slowly mind you, and then produced a small pouch, still moving slow enough to ensure he was not doing anything contrary to simply completing a delivery.

"Here is your item, I did not look in the pouch. It would have done me no good anyway, I am not aware of or know what I am delivering."

The being again did not speak, only watched in an eerie silence as Digger laid the pouch on the table then stepped away after picking up the sack of gold. He stood waiting for the being to check inside the pouch to make sure what was inside was true and authentic, only the stranger made no such move. It stood waiting silently and a little ominously, then Digger finally broke the silence and inquired what was to come next.

"Do you want to check what is inside in the pouch?"

One last time the being never spoke or offered a sound, just pointed with the arm covered in the long glove to the door. Digger knew immediately what was expected and he only nodded once before turning and running from the room. He practically ripped the door off the hinges as he did so happy was Digger for being free from that space and the being in it.

In the room the stranger waited until it knew Digger was gone, as well as the second one who had followed the first idiot. The gloved hands reached up and pulled the cowl of the cloak back and down revealing the handsome face of a lady Red Dragon. She sighed and shook her head sending the long mane of black hair on her head spilling out of the cowl of her cloak.

"Where do they find such dimwitted humans?" She hissed reaching for the pouch on the table.

Her age, just as old as Thaxmosis, benefitted her with special abilities and one of those was an attunement to treasure. She knew the Eye was in the room the moment the fat fool stepped through the door. With a gentle touch she opened the pouch and let the gem rollout into her open hand. Oh it was remarkable, beautiful beyond words, but that was not the reason she wanted the gem. No, she had a deep, resolute need to possess the Eye and no one could know she had it. Why else would she pay for the thieves to steal the diamond/sapphire from Thaxmosis?

"That fool in Thathu had no inclination what you are my lovely. He simply possessed you where I, Balanur, I know just what you were created for. Yes, I know your secret and when we return to my lair our work will begin."

She tucked the eye back into the pouch and then reset her

cowl to hide her face. With the deal complete Balanur left the room and headed off into the dark streets of Thesedell and the night. No one took note of her presence as she moved through the city, much like Digger, the Dragon had learned how to draw little to no attention to her passing.

Epilogue II

Jared sat at the table staring into the bowl of stew but not really seeing the contents of the thick soup, and it had not gone unnoticed by his friend. She sat across the table looking at him knowing full well why he was so depressed now and slightly afraid he may not be able to shake free of the fall. She sipped some of the broth noting it tasted very good, just the right amount of herbs and things, so it was not her cooking that held back his spoon.

"Is the stew too hot?" She asked with a grin.

"No," he responded with a shake of his head, "it is fine, taste very good actually."

"Well that is a comfort, though I do think if you took a taste you might be able to tell me that truthfully."

Caught by his own words, all Jared could do was smile and nod. "You are right Celtis. I am not the best of company at the moment, am I?"

"You certainly are pleasant company, shades more than

being alone." She quickly stated trying to bolster this small turn of emotion. If he could just catch it she thought, take hold of the rising hope and let it carry him out of the dark.

And it did as Jared finally took a spoon full of the stew and then another and one more. Celtis smiled and ate more from her bowl feeling a bit of relief herself when Jared spoke.

"Your father's tome, does it speak much about the Lord of the Paracletus?"

The question was coming, had been ever since the morning he left for the Dragon's lair in Thathu. The answer could either be a tempest in a teapot or a full blown maelstrom she thought. Celtis was the youngest daughter of Cenloth, his leaving this world for some 40 years ago now. Everyone in the small village on the outskirts of the grand Simian city of Gobara knew the recluse Weasel as the kin of the mad historian. It was how Jared ended up on her doorstep one afternoon, holding a medallion in one hand and a boyish grin that could disarm any lady. The villagers eagerly directed the strange being on to her home, feeling at ease to have the tall one who refused to show his face to anyone away from their home, that was until he was alone in her home. When she saw him, took in his full face, Celtis knew he was looking for her father, just 40 years too late. Which is why she sent him on to speak with Thaxmosis, though she never thought he would directly confront the Ancient Dragon, or defeat the creature in hand to hand combat, or bring to her such a wonderful piece of treasure as her father's long lost tome of knowledge.

"It does, so much, and I will read every word to you which he wrote down Jared. All that he knew of the Paracletus I will give to you."

"Even if it tells you my father was...a murderer?" He asked and the mood crept back to a coldness. Celtis slowly lowered her spoon feeling the want to say something to soothe him but also a need to let Jared continue. He looked over to the fire in the hearth which made Celtis cringe inside even more just as he whispered. "Thaxmosis told me my father killed my mother, that he became crazed and stabbed her to death. I was taken from away just in time or he would have killed me as well, just as he killed all the ones who looked up to him."

The words made Celtis chill. She had never liked the story, and that was all it truly was, a story her father used to tell his many children. No one truly knew what had happened that night so long ago, only rumors, tales, and lies seemed to be all anyone could or wanted to tell of that night. The words needed to be addressed though and she did it exactly in the way her father would have done such a task.

"And you believe what the Black Dragon told you? He would not lie to you or manipulate you for his own gain, no, not the 'Terrible One'?" Celtis asked with just a hint of scorn for the Wyrm and Jared's head turned back to face her.

"No...I know Thaxmosis just wanted to hurt me when I refused to tell him the truth."

"Good," she answered quickly with a sad smile, "because even if my father's book says your father was a murderer I will tell you everything. I can say I do not put much faith in the tales gossiped of that night because my father would have told us of such a thing before he passed and he did not. Are you afraid now, though, of what you might find?"

"No," he answered again, quicker this time with more life, "I will never fear what I discover about my father and mother. I could never be afraid to learn what happened to them, but I know now...I will never rest till what happened the night they were taken from this world is known...the truth and not some tale."

He's accepted what might come of opening this door to his past Celtis thought sighing with some relief. "And that is how you should feel because it may take some time to find the truth. My father was an exceptional historian Jared, but it will take us both to find the truth he never could, both of us working together."

Her words again bolstered that small piece of hope he clung to as he nodded. "Thank you Celtis, for your help and knowledge."

"No, thank you for bringing my father back to me. I missed the old cantankerous Weasel."

The remark made him chuckle and Celtis urged him silently to hold onto the emotion. He had to keep climbing out of this dark hole and be that young one who had come asking a hundred questions and all in one breath. Yet the chuckles came to a stop as he smiled with concern back to her, "I knew the Dragon would lie to me and yet I know what he said about my birthright, about being the new Lord was true. I know this from his reaction at seeing the medallion but..."

His last trailed off leaving Celtis a little worried once more. "But what Jared?"

He faltered just a moment before answering, as if Jared were looking for the words and arranging them in his head. "I think I do not wish to be this Dominum Summum, this Lord Supreme. I do not even know who I am yet, how can I be something so...lofty when I felt so much rage for Thaxmosis? How can I be a supreme anything when I do not know what I am...what makes me, me?"

Oh my friend, you are wise beyond your youth. I warned that what you might find when you opened the door to your past may not be what you want and yet you never looked back when you left that morning. "Then you must discover who you are Jared Sinn, see if you are meant to be the true Lord Supreme of the Paracletus or if you were just meant to be...well, just Jared Sinn."

"And how do I do that?" He asked with a chuckle.

Celtis sighed and shook her head, like a mother feeling a little impatient with a child. "By doing exactly what you have done till this very moment, using the mind and the soul you were born with to decide what path you want to walk."

"It is that easy, just choose?"

"Yes it is, choice will always be bound to action and your actions will tell those you meet in your life who you are, so much more than your words." She answered and Celtis could see him turn the words over and over, maybe too much so she decided to give him a nudge. "Like right now, your action of not eating my stew tells me you do not like my cooking."

"No, no," Jared laughed shaking his head, "I am very fond of you cooking. I like it very much!"

"You can say you like it all you want but I do not see you

eating." She countered laughing now herself.

The young Paracletus picked up his spoon and quickly shoveled in two spoons full spilling most on his chin and table as he laughed more. "See, see, I am eating your stew. Oh, it is so good!"

"Stop Jared," Celtis cackled now as she shook her head, "do not make a mess...oh Jared, look at my table!"

The End

About the Author...

R.Kane lives in the Southern US with his family where he was born. He enjoys the occasional fishing trip for bass and throwing the ball with his Golden Retriever. Please visit the website for updates - http://www.rkanepublications.com

www.ingramcontent.com/pod-product-compliance
Lightning Source LLC
Chambersburg PA
CBHW020234180626
46810CB00006B/2179